SOLDIER SAILOR

'Compelling, mundane and funny, *Soldier Sailor* is about the life-and-death business of being a mother and it is a huge, small book. I kept having flashbacks. This is a scorching read. I could not put it down.'

   Anne Enright

'Every woman on earth will identify with this book. Every man will learn something urgent to his betterment. It sings with great authority about the wretched entrapment and molecular joy of motherhood, doing for Irish prose what Eavan Boland did for poetry. A radiant and fearless work of universal import.'

   Sebastian Barry

Claire Kilroy

Soldier Sailor

faber

First published in 2023
by Faber & Faber Ltd
The Bindery, 51 Hatton Garden
London, EC1N 8HN

Typeset by Faber & Faber Ltd
Printed in the UK by CPI Group (UK) Ltd, Croydon, CR0 4YY

*This is a work of fiction. All of the characters, organisations and
events portrayed in this novel are either products of the author's
imagination or are used fictitiously*

A CIP record for this book
is available from the British Library

ISBN 978-0-571-38114-2

Printed and bound in the UK on FSC paper in line with our continuing
commitment to ethical business practices, sustainability and the environment.
For further information see faber.co.uk/environmental-policy

2 4 6 8 10 9 7 5 3 1

For Jim Kilroy; Trambo, Donkey Howthy, Dad
Daddy

And for Sarah Bannan, our wounded soldier
whose beloved sailor, Ruairí, departed this
world. *Go mbeidh áit aige i measc na nAingeal.*

ONE

Well, Sailor. Here we are once more, you and me in one another's arms. The Earth rotates beneath us and all is well, for now. You don't understand yet that what we share is temporary. But I do. I close my eyes and I understand.

Past midnight. I am the only one awake in the house. You cause me such trouble but look at you, just look at you. Delicious, a passing woman once remarked, and I held you a little closer. I tell you all the time that I love you, but it's not enough. *I love you, yes? I love you, okay? I love you, are you listening? Do you understand?* I'll exhaust whatever time we have left together pummelling you with this assertion and never feel I have driven home my point. What is wrong with me?

I push my face into your hair, place my lips on your neck the better to absorb you and it feels stolen. Stolen from whom, I don't yet know. She will reveal herself in good time, in bad time, or maybe it will be a he. They will not be good enough for you and I will smile a brittle smile and keep this knowledge to myself. Whatever it takes to keep you in my life. I am trying to prepare myself. This is me trying to prepare myself.

Do you know what I would do for you? I hope not. What would I not do, is the question. The universe careens around us and I shield your sleeping body with my arms, ready to proclaim to the heavens that I would kill for you: that I would kill others for you, that I would kill myself. I would even kill my husband if it came down to it. I swear every woman in my position feels the same. We all go bustling about, pushing shopping trolleys or whatever, acting like love of this voltage is normal; domestic, even. That we know how to handle it. But I don't.

I'm too old for you. I see that now. Now that it's finally time to grow up. I thought I was young but then you blazed into my life and that was the end of that. I can barely keep up the pace. I try, I do, but it goes hard on me. By the time darkness falls, I can't face my old enemy, the stairs. I slouch there, trying to summon the wherewithal. Yet every night, no matter how wrecked I am, I gaze at your sleeping face. Yes, yes, I know: we scream at each other from morning to night but my love for you swells its banks while you sleep. I murmur it to your sleeping body. Which is no good to you, but still. Here I sit. Have you any idea of your beauty? Photos never quite capture it.

I am worried that one day we won't speak. It happens all the time. You'll turn around some day and blame me for everything. Things that haven't happened yet will be my fault. What I have done and what I have failed to do. And I ask this: that we will always talk. Don't cut me out of your life. One day you will leave and that is as it should be. Part of me cannot wait. And then there's this part. I dreamt that our names were carved upon a stone anchor for all eternity. And in a way they are.

It is late and I am tired. There are things I must tell you. Bad things, dark things, things I have concealed. Your trust is so blind that it hurts. I almost left you once.

A bad confession is worse than none at all. I did leave you. There you were, all alone. The wrongness of this image rears up at me at off-guard moments – when I'm rinsing a cup or putting on a wash, you just lying there with your perfect skin. I wasn't myself. Still amn't. I waited until you were asleep because I could not do it to your face. You would drift off and I would slip away. That was the plan. Later you would wake and look for me but I would not be there, and I would never be there again.

It was our first Easter together. I had been looking forward to the break for weeks. Relying on it, in fact. Big mistake. I was setting myself up for a fall. The dark months of our early days had been more arduous than anything I had ever experienced or even known routinely happened to women in the Western world, dragging myself through the graveyard shift, wounded soldier that I was. But Easter was on the horizon and the longer days signalled that the ordeal was almost over, that we had gotten through it, we had survived, that everything was about to get brighter, warmer, easier, the world was on the brink of bursting into flower, and in this Eden our happiness – oh our *happiness*, Sailor! our clean, white *happiness* – would prevail. If we can just make it to Easter, I coached myself all January, February and March as I inched steadily towards the crevasse. There is always an idealised image in my head of how a thing will

3

be, but it never matches up to the reality.

You are the sole exception.

The discrepancy between my expectations and how Easter panned out made my subsequent dismay vengeful. Self-pity is a dangerous emotion. I should know. I saw in the small hours of Good Friday in a black rage, a malevolent force pacing the corridors of my own home. I was an exhausted woman exhausting myself further and I seem to have broken through some barrier that night because reality ceased to be reality, not that I understood that at the time. To my mind I had experienced a staggering revelation. Namely: I was just a woman. I was just a woman! How had this not registered before? A woman was of less value in this society than a man. A man's time was more important, he had more important things to do. It was now time to step back and let the man do his more important things. No, Sailor, marriage was not what I had anticipated marriage would be. You leave yourself open when you plight your troth to another person. You place your well-being on a level footing with theirs. If they don't meet you halfway, well. Well, well, well, I thought as I stared at the door my husband had shut in my face earlier that night. Well, well, well, it's like that, is it?

When they come, this person you think you want to spend your life with, I will be watching. I will be smiling, teeth bared.

No, I won't. I will be happy for you. You know I will.

Dawn arrived on Good Friday and with it despair – no sleep but I must face the day. Everything felt weird. Weirder than usual: I hadn't had an unbroken night's sleep since you'd exploded onto the scene – I love you, but Jesus wept. If I could just have had six uninterrupted hours to myself, maybe none of this would have happened.

Four. I'd take four. Three.

These are not excuses. There is no excuse. None of this is your fault.

It feels good to talk to you this way all the same. To have this time with you. We are together all day but we never have *time*, if you know what I mean? Of course you don't. You hardly know what time is.

My husband had managed to sleep that night. I had heard him – I had *listened* to him on the other side of that door – snoring away in the box room, those snug, contented snores I used to find endearing, the two of us tucked up together in the same bed on a cold night, except we were no longer in the same room. And soon we would no longer be under the same roof, nor even under the same stars. I could not get my head around it: how could my husband sleep under the circumstances? How was it physically possible? I was too wired to even yawn. Wasn't the adrenaline coursing through his veins too, making him jumpy and wild? I wanted to bellow it at his door: *How can you sleep in there? When you don't know what you will wake to? All bets are off, don't you get it?*

He wasn't even tired. That was the killer. He wasn't the one up every night. I kept slapping the crook of my arm with my hand, like a junkie drumming up veins, to stop myself from doing something stupid. These details are only coming back now. It sounds demented because it was. Up and down I paced outside the box room slapping my arm and sort of panting, sharp shallow huffs as I tried to . . . what? Contain myself? I had never found myself uncontainable before. I had never been afraid of what I might do next. I gasped with the effort of not screaming, of not hurting myself, of not going in there and hurting him. I wanted to so much that I moaned. He should know what he had done to my world. I am just a woman, I rasped over and over in astonishment, hardly able to credit it. My husband had demonstrated this cold, hard truth to me. I wonder whether you can die of resentment, Sailor? Not instantly, but over time. Can it damage cells and trigger cancer? Weaken your heart? There were times when I resented my husband so much, I worried it'd kill me. If I didn't kill him first. Look at him, in there sleeping again. He'd been sleeping all winter. The more he slept, the more I seethed. The more I seethed, the less I slept. I kept blinking in the early days, do you remember that? Sometimes you used to smile and blink back, thinking it was a signal we were exchanging. I was squeezing my eyes shut to try to dispel the murky film that seemed to have built up on them. Nothing dispelled it. I made mental notes to replace the lightbulbs with brighter ones but do you think I could get around to it? It's gone, the murk. It was just exhaustion, the body diverting its energy. Or something. What do I know? Don't listen to me. As I've said, it was an ordeal and I am sorry that at a delicate time in your life the person you needed most was a mess. I got confused once when I caught sight of my coat

6

hanging on the back of a chair in the kitchen. I clapped my hands to my head, wondering how I was over there if I was right here.

'My husband,' I said, stepping back from the box-room door as if I had finally outed the real villain of the piece. It was as great a revelation in its own way as the revelation that I was just a woman. 'My *husband*.' The more I said it, the more peculiar the syllables sounded, until they detached themselves from their original meaning and became the noun describing the changeling that had replaced the man I loved. My *husband*: the enemy within, he who has taken me down. I cocked my head at the door, ears attuned to the snores, thinking: who is this individual? Where did he come from, this *husband* who has seen fit to finish me? Although he had been in my life longer than you, he felt provisional in a way you never could.

Is that wrong?

When my husband woke that morning I felt afraid. Not of him, never of him, but of the next act. It was time. You hardly knew what time was but it was time. He rose promptly when his alarm went off at six thirty but I remained lying in bed, tracking his movements around the house. Showering, eating breakfast, as if it were a day like any other. He was going, of all places, to work. My husband was not expected in the office that day. We had made plans but he was making a point: that his plans no longer included me. The fight the night before had been shocking. I understood that I was in shock. I understood that a lot of pain was coming down the line – the train tracks were humming with it – but that it hadn't kicked in yet. The fight was over you, Sailor. We fought day and night over you. He'd had it, he'd informed me in a voice so unfamiliar it threw me. It was robotic in tone, an automated simulation, but it was coming out of his mouth. I stared at him in fright, witnessing – in my head, at least – a chilling phenomenon: the real man breaking through the facade he had deceived me with. He had sheared off his hair at some point that day, shaved it off himself with the clippers in the garage, a man heading off to war. There he stood, a steely-eyed mercenary in the doorway of the living room, my *husband*, wearing that cut-off hoodie because he'd been training again – he trained fanatically once you came on the scene. What was he training *for*? Night after night he was down in that garage doing whatever it was he did out there, getting leaner, stronger, harder. Defining himself in opposition to me, this wife who had grown weepy and soft. With the knotty arms and the buzz cut, he looked like a thug, an intruder in our home.

'It's like this,' the real him spelled out in no uncertain terms, one hand on the door handle and the other gripping the frame, because he was not about to set foot in the same room as this wife if he could avoid it. He had already moved his belongings to the box room. 'I want you out in the morning. From now on, we communicate through solicitors.'

'That isn't how this works,' was my reply. I blinked and I blinked but it wasn't the murk: my husband's hair was going grey. I had not noticed until that moment. Then, with scathing courtesy, he wished me a good night and shut the door.

I felt no love for him then. I mentally patted my pockets as I slouched on the couch we had picked together that had a *his* and *her* side. Do I love him, I asked myself, and trawled through my body with my mind's eye as if an emotion could be located within the physical self, which, in this case, it could not.

He was so cruel that night. Yet I cannot call my husband a cruel man. I almost did not know him once you entered our lives, no more than I knew myself.

Little by little, the shock wore off.

By midnight, I was frantic. Said all that. By morning, I was resolute.

As soon as the front door closed I sprang from the bed, showered, put on make-up, did my hair, the works, fuelled by a manic energy. I raced through every room in the house, throwing open the curtains. The early morning light was somehow unsound. I was unable for it. The clock had gone forward the weekend before and I felt like I'd crossed several time zones. The dawn light penetrated the rooms in unfamiliar configurations, as if the house had tilted, projecting queer shadows too high up on the walls, and into the recesses of my head, casting light on matters I hadn't noticed before, specifically the ugly side that had been revealed of my husband, and the ugly side that had been revealed of me. My God, we *hated* each other. All along, we had been harbouring these unplumbed reservoirs of *hate* – I cannot tell you what a fright this discovery was. You think you know someone, Sailor. You think you love them. You think they love you. Although I was standing in my own house, I felt myself to be very far from home. If home is a place of safety and sanctuary, then I was as far from it as I had ever been.

I stood by the fireplace biting what was left of my nails. I didn't cry – I was wearing mascara. Our living room and everything in it looked staged, a theatre set. I didn't buy it for a minute.

I ate my breakfast standing up, staring at myself chewing in the mantelpiece mirror. Been a while since I'd seen myself in make-up. An abrupt laugh although nothing was funny. I sounded mad so abruptly stopped, which sounded madder still. I put my cup and bowl in the dishwasher and then fished them back out. I washed them. I dried them. I returned them to the cupboard. Left no trace. My husband's breakfast dishes remained untouched in the sink. He generally cleans up after himself. I'll give him that.

What a treasure. It's so low, Sailor. The bar for men is set so low.

The place was strewn with my belongings, stuff that had gathered there because I had gone beyond sorting it out. Chaos was the medium I inhabited once you entered my life, once you became it. I swiped the chaos into black plastic sacks, dumped the sacks in the boot of the car. Back upstairs to reef all my clothes off their hangers. Seams ripped, buttons pinged. My clothes, some of them beautiful, no longer fit me. Loss of self, loss of self – hard to bear. I bagged them up, out of sight, out of mind. I stuffed that sack into the boot too and blinked at it. Like a dead body, I thought, which it kind of was. I loved those clothes, loved the girl I had been in them, but she was gone. Up the stairs, down, up again, down – I was going about things in a haphazard fashion, making work for myself. Didn't matter. The main thing was to keep moving.

I placed the wedding photograph face down. Stripped the marital bed and put the linen on a boil wash. I hoovered up every trace of myself that I could find, poking the nozzle into corners and behind furniture. So much of my hair. Everywhere I looked there was more of it, a fine tracery veiling the floor the way the murky film veiled my eyes. The amount that had fallen out. I tried not to care. It's just hair, I told myself. Doesn't matter. Don't stop. The train tracks had started to thrum. Something big was coming down the line.

I extracted the bag of hair and dust from the hoover and threw it not in the wheelie bin by the back door but the litter bin at the end of the street. It had rained overnight and I had forgotten to take off my slippers. The wet pavement destroyed the soft soles so I threw them in the bin too and tiptoed back in my socks. I was wild, Sailor, I was out of my mind. I wish I knew where I got the energy. If I did, I would go back and get more.

When I was finished, my house – no, not my house any more – the house was in order. The cushions, they were plumped. The place looked great. I liked that house. It was a good house. No one could pin it on the house. It had surfaces again, polished surfaces reflecting the morning light.

The clean lines of my old life. You don't know what you've got till it's gone. Now there's a lesson only learned the hard way. I missed my old cat all of a sudden, though she was as dead as the girl I used to be. You think you're over something when out of nowhere a tentacle grips you. Skeins of pain unspooling across time: there is no end to it, Sailor. We are walking landmines. My old cat. It's stupid. What I wouldn't have given to feel her warm mass in my arms again. The urgency of that need scared me because I haven't yet lost a person who is close and if this is how bad the death of a cat is? Well. But I didn't cry: the mascara. I stood there, hugging myself. Then I opened all the windows, not sure why. It was time to face you.

When I saw you, I let on that nothing was wrong. I smiled, might have even sung. I wanted you to remember a warm presence, if you would remember me at all. And you responded, you always did. Your capacity for joy is a thing I prize in you, a quality I am determined to protect. You beamed back at me, your innocence recalling that of Ming, my poor cat. You know her, actually – she's the one in the photo. I offered her up to the vet one wet winter evening, holding her down as she struggled to escape, assuring her that everything would be fine while the vet shaved her dainty foreleg and inserted a needle. She was dead within seconds. I hadn't realised it would happen so fast. I thought she would fade away peacefully in my arms while I murmured to her that she was the best, most loving and loyal cat ever – while I thanked her, essentially, while I told her all the things she deserved to be told – but no, she flopped on the table and banged her head. I gathered her up and she seemed to be looking at me, staring out in panic from her paralysed body. 'Is she still alive?' I asked the vet in horror. 'Is she still alive?' I asked again when he didn't answer. He reached out and closed her eyes with the sweeping gesture of a hypnotist.

I'm always the one asking stupid questions. The world seems so much clearer to everybody else. I have no aptitude for the practicalities of this life. What can I possibly offer you?

Nothing. Everything. The whole of my heart.

I carried my dead darling through the packed waiting room that had terrorised her only minutes earlier, wiping my eyes and nose with the back of my hand as I paid the bill. I drove home with her curled up on the passenger seat growing cold and stiff and somehow hollow, and it was desperate, Sailor, so desperate, so grim, not the way to end things after all that I owed her. We set out in life believing we will forge so many enduring bonds when really we are blessed with so few, no more than three or four if we are lucky, and one of mine was with a cat. The only bond she got to forge was with me and she gave that her all. Ming was old and suffering and her kidneys were failing. Putting her to sleep was the merciful thing to do. Birth, death – you only get one shot. I got her death wrong and I cannot make it right. I know I'm talking about what I did to her to avoid talking about what I did to you but she sprang to mind when I saw you that morning because she had blindly trusted me too.

Around eleven, the pair of us headed out together. It was an unusually lovely day, or maybe it was just a normal one but I had acclimatised to everything being dire. It had been a harsh winter, the coldest on record apparently, but don't they say that every year? This was the coldest winter, that was the wettest spring, here comes an apocalyptic summer. I threw a blanket into the car to be safe. The back seat was jammed with the bin bags that wouldn't fit in the boot. I couldn't see out of the rear-view mirror as I reversed.

I knew where I wanted to bring you – I had given it some consideration the night before and chosen the cliff path for its beauty, a place you might want to return to some day after the dust had settled – and then we were in one another's arms once more. I held onto you for too long and not long enough. I should never have let you go. Nothing in my life had ever felt so good. The world rotated beneath us and we were the world. You did not yet understand that what we shared was temporary, that it was in fact drawing to an end. But I did.

I closed my eyes and I understood.

* * *

Your dear head resting in the crook of my arm. Me, treasuring its weight. My thumb stroking your cheekbone, your temple, your brow. The blanket outspread on the verge beneath us; the warmth of the sun on our skin. I understood then why people used to smile when they saw us. We were beautiful together, you and I. We were the most beautiful thing I had ever been part of. You studied me for a beat before smiling up and you may as well have driven hot skewers through my sinuses, such was the pain of biting back tears. I bent down and laid a Judas kiss upon your forehead.

Neither of us made a sound. You smiled again but you were getting drowsy. I was in something of a trance myself. I rocked gently, humming a nothing tune. The world kept turning and the sun got in your eyes. They squinted shut. I leaned forward to shade your face. Your eyes opened again. A smile. Shut again. I should have brought a pair of scissors, I thought foolishly, to steal one of your curls. Then your sweet body was falling and I was catching it. No one had ever drifted off in my arms until you.

Your breathing slowed and by and by you were gone. It was like death, Sailor. It was as if you had died.

I stopped rocking you in this awful afterlife but you did not wake. I said your name. I said it twice. I threw back my head. No, you would not remember me. How had I thought you might?

It was time. You hardly knew what time was but soon you'd find out. The rails were zinging by then and they are zinging again now because I am coming to the bad bit. I took out my phone. He still hadn't called. My husband had wanted to punish me? Well. Before he had started in on me, I had never felt as lost in my life. By the time he was finished, I had stepped off the bottom rung and set foot in an underworld where everything was inverted. I don't want to trouble you with that place. I powered down the phone and slotted the

15

thin slab into my pocket. I was really doing this. This was really happening.

I extricated myself from your sleeping body and delicately laid your delicate head down. I arranged the blanket around you and stood back. There you were, your own republic, a sovereign state. This key moment in your history was unfolding but you would never have access to it. I had bequeathed you a blank page.

Now what? I didn't know. I hadn't thought that far ahead. We were both stuck on the same blank page. I stepped forward to adjust the blanket around you again, willing you to wake up because that would have stopped me. I could never have left you with the image of me turning my back on you. Though in my head, I was not turning my back on you. I was saving you. From me, from how bleak I felt, from that bleakness contaminating you. I've said it before, somewhere: depression is contagious. It leaps from one person to the next. Someone would love you, someone would always love you, and she would love you better than me. I left you so that another woman could love you better. More safely, is what I mean. That was the truth of it. Please, I begged, but to whom and for what, I still can't say.

I stared at the sun. My retinas winced but I brazened it out, squinting at the blazing light through trembling slits, burning off that murky film – or burning it on as it turned out – because when I looked down at you again, you were suspended over a floating hole. Dark shapes throbbed across you, obscuring your face. I blinked to get you back but you were gone. Off I stumbled with a choked noise, baited by those drifting shadows, which were general now, a swarming legion. So this is chaos, I remember thinking. This is the end of days.

A rolling chasm opened up wherever my gaze landed and I pitched towards the void without ever quite reaching it. Two songs were entangled in my brain. *I didn't mean to hurt you. I'm sorry that. I never meant to cause you any sorrow.* I tore at my marriage rings until the knuckle cracked, but no joy. Those things were soldered onto me. I despised my husband then, I *despised* him, but I loved you more than I'd known it possible to love. In my mind I was performing an act of love. The most loving thing I thought I could do for you was to rid you of me. To set you free.

I didn't mean to. I never meant to cause you. Or make you cry. All the time gasping for air as if I'd just surfaced from the depths, when really I was descending into them. The Virgin Mary, of all people, came to mind. I ask blessed Mary, ever virgin. Having never given her a moment's consideration in my life, it then struck me that she was real. Not real as in there beside me – don't worry, I wasn't having a visitation – but real as in there had once been a girl, a living girl, a child in fact, called Mary, Maryam, Mariam; a child who had given birth in a stable at the age of thirteen or fourteen or possibly twelve. Where was her mother, was my question. Where was the poor kid's *mother*? How could you let your child go through that without being by her side? Unless you had been so brutalised yourself that it

17

seemed normal. Childbirth, let me tell you, is no joke. And that wasn't the worst of it. Her darkest hour was yet to come. This motherless mother had to watch her son being whipped and mocked and stabbed and crucified – *nailed to a wooden cross* – and there was not a thing she could do to stop it. She couldn't even hold her child's hand. She was there on Good Friday, she stayed by her boy's side, watched them hammer nails through his dear feet and wrists while he addressed himself to his father in the sky, who was absent. It was easier to be the son on the cross than the mother at his feet, because she would have given anything, anything, to have taken his place. I know this. There is nothing a mother would not do to protect her child from harm. She would kill others for him, she would kill her husband, she would kill herself. Mary suffered more than her child, and for longer. She suffered the horror of her child's suffering until her dying day.

I feel sick. I feel physically sick at the prospect of harm coming to you. Where are they, those who would hurt you? Line them up. I'll take them out one by one.

I was in a forest by then. There was heat in the sun, but I was cold. All winter you had kept me warm. Your absence was an amputation. There was a shivery patch where we had been conjoined. He's free, I told myself, I have freed him, now he is free. You would always be loved. You will always be loved. At night, I touch your face with my thoughts. Could I pick out your hand from a thousand hands? Yes, I could! You saved me. I'm sorry, I'm jumping ahead. This is muddled. So am I.

I followed my jagged shadow. We lurched across uneven

ground. Spring, birds singing, an early bumblebee, the ones you always worry will get too cold and die. Those tender, almost transparent – translucent is what I mean – those translucent new leaves on the trees: they had probably only unfurled that morning. My sight must have been restored by then because I acutely remember those leaves. I stopped to look up at them shimmering, all kinds of emerald, back-lit by the sun, and we had waited so long for spring that I wanted you to see the baby leaves too; I turned to point them out to you, but oh, oh. I zigzagged like a drunk from tree to tree, pockets rattling. A swathe of bluebells hovered like mist above the grass. Ferns, the scent of three-cornered leeks. The forest got deeper, and I got deeper into the forest, trying to hide my contorted face. 'You're free,' I said, 'I have freed you,' because I was talking out loud by then. '*I never meant. I'm sorry that.* Oh, oh.'

I encountered a mound of briars. It was as high as my chest and tore at my jacket as I attempted to wade through it. I heard fabric ripping and was gratified by the sound. Look at me! I suppose was my logic. Behold my suffering. I was with-out my anchor, our names carved in stone. You don't need to hear this. Which is why I wait until you're asleep.

I got caught before I made it halfway across – of course I did – and when I tried to turn, a hundred hooks snagged my legs out from under me and down I went on my back, top-pling like a statue off a plinth. I let myself fall. I was ready to come to a stop. The jittery energy drained from my body as if a plug had been pulled. I was done. I started to cry, in shame as much as anything, on my bed of tiny nails. A grown woman stuck in a bush. The girl I used to be would never have blah blah. I tried to wipe my nose but my sleeve was caught in the thorns, so I lay there snivelling up at the sky, pegged down like a tent.

I grew calm as I abided there with the other wild animals. After a time the forest absorbed me into it and I was grateful. It was more than gratitude: I was moved. That these wood-land creatures should accept me into their domain was just so . . . it was just so . . . tears again. I loved them, those creatures, I felt an abrupt but powerful kinship with them. Birdsong, squabbles on branches, the drone of insects – the volume crept back up. Wood pigeons re-embarked on their conver-sations. They were probably talking about me. A breeze was weaving through the canopy. Always loved that sound. I gazed at the leaves for a spell, the world happening up there without me, until it became abstract and I got confused, to be simultaneously lying on Earth and drifting away from it, to be at a remove while it held me up. Wasn't it lovely, though, our green planet, now that I had a moment to contemplate it – those leaves, that sound, the intricacy of air currents, every last thing in flux. I was finally alone, it came to me then. *Alone* alone. Alone as in how we face death. Green is my favourite colour, I thought, gazing at its many variations. I hadn't had time to think in so long. My world had become too calamitous. A balance, the great balance I hadn't realised was suspended over me all along, had tipped. I was sliding off. Plus I had forgotten to drop the bin bags to the clothing bank.

And you, abandoned and irresistible, just waiting for another woman to take you in her arms. A flare of jealousy. I closed my eyes but I didn't understand.

I'm sorry that. I never meant. A creature was approaching in speculative bursts across the forest floor. I tracked its progress without opening my eyes. A bird? Too loud. It got closer still, then stopped to regard the felled giant in its midst. Fox? Rat? That's when something pronged my scalp. I launched up and out of there with a shriek, by which time the creature had fled.

On the other side of the briars was a lush clearing of grass, lanced with sunlight and still as a rock pool. No human had set foot there in years. It was a glorious little glade and I immediately thought of you: hey look! But oh, oh. I was so tired, so beyond myself. Mother Mary, come to me. But who was there for her? Who mothered the mothers? Weren't mothers people too? Weren't they the ones on the hardest station of all? I took the tub of pills out of my pocket and tipped a few onto the palm of my hand.

I'd left my bottle of water in the car.

Stepping on the moss-green carpet detonated a booby trap of screeching. Birds sprang into life at my intrusion, a pair of them, flapping and shrieking. They appeared to be shrieking at *me*. I shooed them away but they wouldn't desist. They had lost their minds too. 'Jesus,' I said to them, 'what is the problem?' It was a crazy little pocket I had happened upon. Then I saw it.

There on the forest floor, purplish pink among the vivid

greens, and just about heavy enough to bend the grass, was a
foetus. It was no larger than my big toe and at first I thought
it *was* a big toe. 'Fuck,' I cried as I twisted to avoid stepping
on it, which put the wind up the birds. Don't stop, I warned
myself, but I had already stopped. Don't look, but I had
already bent over.

Unviably large head, purple body all elbows, bulbous eye-
lids sealed shut and a yellow beak. The merest membrane of
skin. A hatchling.

The birds ramped up their protest. 'What do you want me
to do?' I asked them. 'It's dead.' I gesticulated at the unfor-
tunate scrap. 'Your baby is dead.' I don't know why I was so
callous about it. My mind was reeling. The tablets had lodged
in my throat.

And then it moved. The hatchling opened its beak. Gasping for air or food or life. Birth and death. Was it suffering?
Should I put it out of its misery? Step on it? 'Oh Christ,' I
said to the birds, 'where's your nest?'

I squinted up again at the forest canopy. But how could
I climb a tree? Even without the stitches, I could not have
climbed a tree. So I burst into tears again. It was you there,
Sailor, dying in the grass with no one to help you because
everything vulnerable was you, everything tender was you
those days, and these days, and very possibly all my days. The
screeching seemed shriller than before, though we appeared
to be down to one bird now. The dowdy one, the female. The
male and his glossy sheen had shagged off and the female
was beside herself. I reflexively looked around for someone

to help but I was deep in the forest, Sailor. I was lost.

I knelt down to pick up the hatchling to . . . what? Give it back to the mother? Here is your dying chick? Just before I made contact with it, she dive-bombed me. The mother actually dive-bombed me. I sat back on my hunkers in surprise and admiration. So slight, so drab, so courageous. She put me to shame. I stood up and backed off and she alighted in front of her young, setting herself and her pattering heart between us.

Babies die, I thought as I regarded her. That is the world we live in.

I did not make this world.

If I could, I thought, I would make a different world. I would make a different world for you and me, Sailor. And for this brave bird.

But I can't.

I closed my eyes but I didn't understand.

Demanding where Mary's mother was that night was more of it. Mary had a father too. Where was Mary's father the night his child gave birth in a stable? Where was the hatchling's father? Why did the burden fall on us, the females, with our ruptured bodies?

And then I heard it, clear as a bell: a baby's cry.

'Oh!' I whimpered and covered my mouth. That pain again, the hot skewers.

I whipped around. No sign of a baby. I lowered my hands. 'Where are you?' I called in a sing-song voice so as not to alarm it. Like the baby was going to tell me. Like it would issue directions.

23

There was silence for a beat as the baby considered my voice, then it cried again, its wailing redoubled, the short *a-wah, a-wah* cries of tiny lungs, the type that do something, that loosen something in my core.

'Where are you?' I sang again through a false smile, faking calmness though my heart was racing. The baby had cried right in my ear, but when I had turned, there was no baby. There was no baby in the crazy forest glade.

'I'm coming,' I called, and the baby wailed. But where was the baby? Had I stepped on an unmarked grave? Desperate things happened to newborns in the past, desperate secrets were buried by desperate women. And desperate girls.

I had to go back. But which way was back? The bird screeched and brandished her wings, taking me on with her artillery of feathers while I hunted for a way out. The baby was crying again, the baby was scared. I was crying again, I was scared. I had never heard a frightened baby before and the frequency released something chemical. I had to comfort the baby, calm the baby, make the baby stop crying. I had to hold the baby, and I mean I *had* to, and right now. It was the most extraordinary compulsion I have known. I *had* to hold that baby to my chest, to my cheek, to my skin, to my soul, and rock it until it stopped crying, oh, oh.

And then the baby did stop crying, which was worse. Why had the baby fallen silent? What had happened to the baby?

I located the lowest section of the brambles and tore through them, emerging at the top of a gentle slope. I did not remember being at the bottom of a gentle slope on the way there. The baby cried out and I pushed on, chanting *I don't know what to do, I don't know what to do* as if someone might guide me, but I had made my bed.

I scoured the drifts of wild garlic for my tracks but found no trace. I broke into a run but was I getting closer or further away? It was dismaying, how little ground I covered. Like running up the down escalator. Up until a few months ago, I had regarded myself as young and fit. And up until a few months ago, I was. A dead tree lay propped against another at a diagonal. Had it been there earlier? Of course it had been there earlier, but had I? Had I come that way? I did not remember that tree. But then, what did I remember? Black shapes, floating voids, the end of days. 'Where are you?' I sing-songed to the baby.

No response.

In the distance, a dog was barking. I wouldn't ordinarily have tuned into a barking dog but this was a sustained bombardment. The dog was agitated. Something was agitating the dog. I rerouted to follow the sound. The trees thinned out onto open ground. The dog was still barking. I ran, I tripped, I got up, I ran harder. The breeze whipped my hair down my throat and I gagged. Then I heard the baby again, not up close any more but distant, as distant as the dog. 'I'm coming,' I shouted across the meadow.

I ran for that baby, Sailor. I ran until I thought my heart would burst and then I ran more. I had not known I could run so fast, nor for so long. I'm sure I damaged stitches. 'I'm coming,' I bellowed, careening over the hill like a Viking.

A swish of blonde ponytail on the other side of the hedgerow. There was a woman with the dog. Her head dipped out of sight. No. She was reaching for the baby. No, no, just no.

When she reappeared, it was not the baby in her arms but the barking dog, a stump of writhing muscle. I came plunging out of the undergrowth and there at the foot of a stone bench was the baby, sensational among the greens and sandy greys. I swept up the blue bundle. It was no bigger than a violin and not much heavier.

The baby abruptly stopped crying as its surprised eyes found mine. 'Oh!' I gasped when I saw the beauty of the little face. Look at you! I would have exclaimed if I could speak but I could hardly breathe. Or stand. I sat down hard on the stone bench.

The baby stared at me a moment longer and then howled, and I mean *howled*, at which point the dog lost its shit altogether. It was all the woman could do to keep it in her arms.

'Are you alright?' the woman wanted to know. She had to yell to make herself heard over the dog. The racket was not helping with the baby.

'I'm fine,' I shouted back, though this was patently not the case. I was not fine and the baby would not be fine in my care. I rocked the howling parcel in the crook of my arm and, when that didn't work, I propped him against my shoulder and rubbed his back, my lips at his ear. 'Shush, little darling, shush.'

Which also did not work. So small, so angry.

I looked up. The woman was standing over me. 'Are you sure you're alright? Are you sure that baby is alright?'

I pushed rats' tails out of my eyes and nodded: 'I'm sure.' Sweat was trickling out of my hair and snaking down my face. 'Thank you,' I added to let her know that I had it from here. When she showed no sign of budging, I stood up and pushed past her down the track, making a production of shielding the screaming baby from her barking dog. 'Shush, babba, God, please shush.'

The woman trailed me. I picked up speed. She picked up speed too. I went as fast as I dared go bearing such a precious cargo.

'Excuse me, hello? Hello, excuse me? Are you alright?'

I hurried along as best as I was able. Yes, I'm alright, or would be if you'd just back off. She put on a spurt and overtook me, then planted herself across the path to force me to a stop. She was in her late forties, trim, dressed in a gilet and sports leggings, evidently in control of her life, evidently enjoying it, and maybe wrath is too strong a word for what I felt then but I can't think of any other.

'I want to help,' she told me with a big sincere expression, reaching for my shoulder. The dog, now secured on her hip by just one arm and bulling to get at us, saw its opportunity and lurched. 'Jesus!' I recoiled, and the woman wheeled away and set the dog down, dealing it a sharp yank of the collar. I cupped the back of the baby's bawling head and tucked his hot face into the crook of my neck, or tried to. The baby did not wish to be tucked. The baby was beside himself. The woman remained stooped over the barking dog, holding it by its collar. She did not appear to have a lead.

'Your dog is scaring my baby!' I shouted. 'He is scaring my baby, and he is scaring me!'

At the anger in my voice, the dog's barking morphed into something sinister, something snarling and wolfish. Then, for a brief interlude, we all let rip on the cliff path. 'Stop it!' the woman was shouting at the dog as I shouted at her to make it stop, but the dog didn't stop, and nor did the baby, who was only getting started. In the midst of the uproar, the sun went in and the world turned flat and grey.

Wallop. The dog got it hard across the bridge of the nose. It yelped and collapsed on its back, raising its paws in supplication and exposing a pink belly nubbled with prominent nipples. Another female, possibly one that had recently nursed pups but I am no authority on dogs. I can't say bitch, Sailor, I won't say bitch. And nor should you.

The baby, now purple, was screaming at full throttle, his eyes squeezed shut and his tongue curled in spasm in his ridged and gummy mouth. I pressed my lips against his ear so that he might hear if not my voice (inaudible over his howls) but the vibration of it, its muffled thrum. 'Poor little darling,' I murmured, 'poor little babba,' but it was no good. He freed a fist from the blanket and held it clenched in the air like a revolutionary, then arched his back in the grip of what appeared to be some class of fit. Something bad was happening to the baby. I glanced at the woman. She looked alarmed too.

A plastic ring protruded from the folds of the blanket. I fished it out and a soother emerged. I inserted it into his distraught mouth.

It was like putting the pin back into a grenade. The explosion was sucked back in. '*Mmm, mmm, mmm,*' the baby said as his body gave way and curled into mine. He issued a few more protest cries before pushing his face into my neck and rootling there for comfort. '*Mmm, mmm, mmm.*' It was the loveliest feeling, to be the one he turned to. 'That's better,' I crooned, kissing his velvety head before raising my eyes to the woman: See? We are fine. Everything is fine.

While she deliberated, now down on her hunkers to keep hold of her supine dog, I set off again down the track. 'Wait,' she called, but I wasn't stupid. I hurried along with the baby's head cradled under my chin, my shoulder braced for her hand to alight on it once more. If I could just make it back to the car.

I lowered the baby to steal a glance at him. His normal colour was returning. My God, what a beauty – I buried his face in my neck again. I had yanked a Goya off the wall and legged it. I could hardly believe my luck. Still can't.

I looked over my shoulder. The woman was on her phone crouched over the dog, now back on its feet and asphyxiating itself against its collar. If that dog had been a Labrador, an obliging, gormless Labrador, the woman would have the baby. The baby would be in her arms right now. And my arms would be empty.

But the dog was a terrier so my arms were full and that's how they would stay. I laughed. Relief. Insanity. Insanity. Relief. The gods had blinked. The world was different to the one I had set out in that morning, oh about a million years ago. I was the vessel bearing the infant to safety, I was Air Force One. The sun – even the sun – had come back out to acknowledge the glory. 'Almost there,' I assured the baby. 'Almost home.'

It seemed to take longer getting back than it had going out but eventually I rounded the corner and there was my car. It had waited for me, my black steed, so noble, so loyal. My love spilled over for the car. My love spilled over for my surroundings in general. I had so much love, all of a sudden, to bestow. Relief. Insanity. Insanity. Relief.

I couldn't remember how to drive. Steering wheel, handbrake, gear stick, clutch – I touched each of them in turn while speaking their names in an effort to orientate myself. My hands were shaking. The baby cried. Oh God. I turned around but it was only that his soother had fallen out. I thrust myself into the back seat to plug it back in and noticed, through the rear windscreen, that the woman and dog were catching up. I sat back into the driver's seat and took the wheel. I breathed, I composed myself, I tried to look normal. The keys. Start with the keys. I twisted them in the ignition and the engine came to life. I pushed the car into gear, strapped on my seatbelt and drove back into my life.

* * *

The house was cold by the time I made it home – I'd forgotten to close the windows. I ran around shutting them, the baby in my arms. I drew the curtains too, although it wasn't yet dark. You're hiding, I realised as I stole around my own home: I had stowed the car in the garage and smuggled the baby in through the back door.

I brought the baby into the living room and laid him down on the hearth rug. He watched as I assembled logs and kindling in the stove. I struck a match and held up the flame. 'This is fire,' I said. It seemed important to talk to him, to tell him things. I touched the matchstick to the firelighter and the flame leapt across. 'Fire means that you are warm, it means that you are safe.'

Another lie. Fire means danger. Fire means run. Fire means an agonising death.

I gathered the baby up and clasped his small body to my chest. I would save him. I would run into the burning building and carry him out. Whatever it took.

When had it all become so life and death?

Behind the glass door of the stove, the fire caught. Soon the room glowed. The house that had looked fake that morning was now our refuge. I was coming down from a high, or up from a low; either way I was approaching equilibrium again. My hands no longer shook.

I set about undressing the baby. It made me sad, the care with which he had been wrapped earlier that day. He had been dressed for someone else's eyes, each layer an entreaty to whoever found him: this child was treasured, please treasure him again. The blanket was blue lambswool with a single white star on it to indicate that this was not a case of deprivation, like in the old days, of worrying about another mouth to feed. Making it a case of what?

I unfastened the mother-of-pearl buttons on the tiny matinee jacket with trepidation. But the baby was perfect, and apparently perfectly happy. He gurgled at me and kicked his legs. His nappy, though swollen, hadn't soaked through to his babygrow. So he hadn't been left out there as long as I feared. Maybe he had slept through the whole thing and only just woken when the dog started to bark. But maybe he had been crying for his mother for ages, lying on his back staring into the vast emptiness of the sky. And maybe when her face failed to appear he feared, like the hatchling, that he might never make it back to his nest. The baby I had snatched from the ground was a frightened one. Had the ordeal rocked his foundations? It had rocked mine.

There was a letter in the swaddle. A watermark of tears on the envelope. The mother had wanted the baby to some day see those tears and forgive her. I opened the stove and tossed the letter into the fire.

* * *

It was late by the time my husband made it home. The days were getting longer but my husband was getting home later, as if pushing his arrival time forward in small increments would keep me from noticing that he was shirking his duties. My husband must think I am stupid.

There was a time he used to rush home to me, Sailor. A time before you.

He found the two of us on the fireside rug, not a light on in the house. He flicked the switch and I winced.

'Oh, sorry,' he said, switching the light back off. 'I didn't know you were home. I didn't see the car.'

'I parked in the garage.'

'What about my—' he began, but dropped it. What about my gear, he wanted to ask, the gym equipment that had suddenly appeared. It had juddered across the concrete as I drove the car through it like a snowplough, clearing it from my path.

My husband put his laptop case down and crossed the floor to look into your face. 'How's my little man?'

You raised your eyes to his and smiled. 'He's perfect,' I said.

My husband reached down to pick you up but I stiffened around you: *Mine*. A beat, then he retreated empty-handed. 'I was trying to ring you.'

'My phone is off.'

'Oh.' He turned on one of the table lamps and glanced around. 'The place looks different.'

'I tidied it.'

'Wow, it looks great!'

The false cheer. He waited for me to reply. I didn't.

'So, what did you guys get up to today?'

I smirked.

'What?' Smiling expectantly, wanting in on the joke.

'We went for a walk.'

'Good, that's good! You need to get out of the house more. It'll do you both good!'

'Will it?' I asked grimly. I had been launched into outer

33

space and seen how bleak it was out there. I looked up at my husband and realised that he could never understand that place.

'My God, what happened to your face?'

I touched my cheek. 'What's wrong with it?'

'It's all scratched.'

'Just some brambles.' My husband had wanted to punish me? Well.

'Oh sweetheart!' He got down on his hunkers and put a finger under my chin to tilt my face towards his. 'Are you okay?'

He was demonstrating how caring he was, that he was such a caring guy. I turned my face away. 'I'm fine.'

'You look like you've been dragged backwards through bushes,' he remarked. 'But in a cute way,' he hastily added, fearful of saying the wrong thing. He patted my shoulder and ruffled my hair and performed a series of similarly fond twitches to reassure himself that everything was normal, domestic, whatever. 'Look,' he finally said, 'I'm sorry about last night.'

I shrugged without taking my gaze from the fire.

'I'm sorry for those things I said. I was angry. You know I didn't mean them, right?'

You know I didn't mean them, right? What I had almost done for something he didn't mean.

My husband was still speaking but I was no longer listening. I could not possibly have heard your cries in the forest, I knew. But I did hear your cries, Sailor. You woke and you

34

cried out for me and I heard you, clear as a bell. We are joined, you and I, our names on the stone anchor. When one of us dies, the other will feel the loss always.

'Did you hear me?' my husband asked, not unkindly.

I looked at him. 'What?'

'Your cardigan's inside out. Poor silly thing.' Then a tentative, 'What's for dinner?'

When he wandered off in search of something to eat, I scooped you up. I held your head in my open hands and studied you like a book. From my fingertips to my elbow, that's how small you were then. Birth, death. You only get one shot. Sailor, if I could have one wish granted, it would be to do it all over again. I do not want another baby, that is not what I am trying to say. What I want is to do it all over again with you. Except this time getting it right.

But I didn't get it right. I had my chance. And I blew it.

I love you. You're perfect. But I'm not.

A wind had risen at the window. The hatchling was out there, the dowdy female too, warding off rats, foxes, the ghosts of dead babies in unmarked graves. All that anguish heaped on feathers and hollow bones. I shivered and put another log on the fire.

She was a blackbird. It took me a while to figure that out because she wasn't black, she was brown. Designed to blend into the background, I suppose. Her species should be called brownbirds and you should bear my surname and I should bear my mother's because the male . . . oh Sailor, where is the male? When things get ugly, where does he go? I felt certain when I was pregnant that you were a girl, and I practised the things I would tell you throughout your gestation to prepare you for a man's world. Then you appeared and I don't know what to say to you except don't be one of them.

TWO

I opened my eyes. You can sleep standing up. Another lesson learned the hard way. I'd been back in that dream, that hideous dream I used to get about you, when your father asked whether I was going to it.

'To what?' I responded in mild alarm. What had I forgotten this time? And why had I come to the fridge? You were on my hip. You were always on my hip. My body had twisted to adapt to your weight like those windblown trees that grow by cliffs. My belly button still isn't central.

'To that.' He tapped the flyer held to the fridge door by a magnet. The primary colours of the Baby and Toddler Group – toy blocks, handprints, ABCs – images that are patronising, now that I think about it, given the target audience is not the infant but the adult who brings the infant along, the invariably female adult. 'I thought you said you were bringing him to that.'

'What day is it?'

'Thursday.'

'Oh.' *Every Thursday morning!* said the flyer. 'The bins have to go out.'

'You should bring him to that,' concluded the Child Developmental Specialist. 'Socialise him,' he added, a word he had picked up from me.

I had been talking about socialising you at the Baby and Toddler Group for weeks although now apparently it was his idea. Problem was I couldn't get out of the house on time. It was difficult to explain the obstacles to my husband because they weren't obstacles he recognised. They weren't obstacles I'd recognised before having you, the whole three-steps-forwards, two-steps-back racket. Since becoming mobile, you could undo faster than I could do.

It wasn't yet fully bright outside. My husband was already dressed, his hair damp from the shower. I was still in my pyjamas. 'Em.' I opened the fridge and stared at the contents, hoping for a clue. They were sockets, my eyes. Two hot holes bored into my skull. 'I feel more tired than when I went to bed.'

'Bad night?'

Silly question. All nights were bad. Your father still slept in the box room. 'I just don't feel able for today.'

'I'm sorry, honey.'

'I need to get some work done. Maybe when you're home, you can do his bedtime?'

'I'm working late again.'

Yes, the office. His suit, his tie. My pyjamas, my post-partum body. A roll of flab for my role of flab. *Engage the core*, the ab app exhorted me. What did that even mean?

Still no idea why I'd come to the fridge. I swung the door shut again.

'Milk,' my husband reminded me.

I pulled the door open and handed him the milk.

'Jesus Christ, is that all that's left?'

'Sorry.' Milk was my responsibility.

Schlep schlep in my slippers, a slab of flab crossing the floor. I tried to lower you into your high chair but you screamed and clung on, monkey baby. I took you back onto my hip. 'That hurts, darling,' I said, untangling my hair from your fingers.

'Here's your tea.' My husband held out the cup. He could see my hands were full.

'Thanks. Leave it on the counter.'

'Put him down.'

'I can't.'

I could feel him taking me in – the pyjamas, the unwashed hair, the ineffectiveness. 'I'm not incompetent,' I told him. 'I'm exhausted. There's a difference.'

'I didn't say you were incompetent.'

'You didn't have to.'

'I'm just saying: put him down.'

'And I'm just saying: I can't.'

'Of course you can put him down.'

'I *can't*. I can't listen to him scream. I literally *can't*. It scrambles my brain. You don't understand.'

'No, I don't. He's a baby. Babies scream.'

'How about you put him into the chair?' I angled you around to face him. You reached out to your dadda.

He gestured at his suit. You were a barfer, Sailor, a dry-cleaning hazard. He glanced at his phone. 'I've got to go to work.'

'Lucky you,' I remarked flatly.

39

'What's that supposed to mean?'

'At least you *can* go. At least you *can* work.'

'Man goes to work. What a bastard.'

'I can't do my work any more.'

'No one's stopping you.'

I gesticulated at you.

'So get up earlier. Get up at five.'

I thought I might burst into tears at that. The membrane was thin that day. The membrane between coping and not. But I'm so tired! I wanted to weep. 'You get up at five,' I said instead.

I followed him out to the hall, *schlep schlep*. He put on his new navy wool coat. The three of us in the hall mirror. You, me and Hugo Boss. We no longer looked like a married couple. What's he doing with *her*?

'Bye bye, Dadda,' I said on your behalf, waving your little hand. Your father kissed us both before closing the door, a guillotine severing me from my world. Which is not to say that your father was my world, but that he was free to roam in my world, which we should now call his world, or perhaps *the* world, an adult place from which I'd been banished. Now I lived in your world. It was small.

I had missed my window for a shower. I had missed it yesterday too. Whenever yesterday was. You started to grizzle. *Schlep schlep* back down the hall. Seven thirty-five. Thirteen more hours to go.

* * *

I sorted the washing into three piles. The whites, the coloureds, the dark wash. The coloureds had it by a nose. All your bright babygrows and sleep sacks. I stuffed them into the washing machine. To entice you off my hip, I'd set you up with those purple detergent capsules, the ones that look like big jellies.

That's a joke. I'd given you the bottle of bleach.

Relax. You had your cars, okay? I'm not saying I was a great mother but I did my best. You're alive, aren't you?

I went through each item of laundry, pretreating the stains. So many stains, none of them mine. Word of advice: don't leave all your washing to your partner. I couldn't bear for anyone to resent you. Especially someone under your own roof. You might be murdered in your bed.

Though you won't. It's the women who are murdered.

I read the dosage instructions and still didn't know whether the water in my area was hard or soft.

You were learning free will that day. The very thing I was losing, you were gaining in inverse proportion, your independence premised on dismantling mine. You threw down a car and whined. I tossed your elephant top into the machine, set off the wash, and picked you up. 'Okay, darling, let's have breakfast.'

I tried again to insert your legs into the high chair and again you shrieked and this time yanked my hair. 'Ow!' I objected. In your fist, a thin lock, which we both frowned at. I had already lost so much hair. Already threadbare. You took your soother out of your mouth and stuffed my hair in instead.

I tried to get breakfast ready with you on my hip, but it involved kettles and microwaves and your flossy head lunging forward at intervals to get a better look. So I deposited you out of harm's way on the playmat and scattered a few toys around you.

You screamed and the toys were sent flying. You screamed while I stirred and buttered and poured, while I gulped the tea my husband had left on the counter. Normally I would have relented and picked you up but I'd had it after the hair incident. I had had it that morning as I had had it every morning and every afternoon and every evening since you were about six months old, since it had dawned on me that this was my life now, this was freelance motherhood: struggling to contain your screams while struggling to contain my own, which were louder and angrier and scared us both.

Your screaming rose an octave. I clapped my palms to my burning eye sockets and then to my ears. 'Shut up!' I was suddenly yelling, 'just shut the fuck up!' I had had it so then you did it. You were up on all fours. You tilted your head back before walloping it hard against the floor.

The sound was like a watermelon dropping from a height. No: the sound was like a baby's skull hitting a tiled floor. My baby's skull. Which wasn't even closed yet, which still had a soft spot at the crown, your fontanelle; further reminder, where none was needed, of your fragility.

You howled as you lined yourself up to do it again. I sprang forward and inserted my slippered foot. Your head came down on it with some force. You weren't kidding

42

around, Sailor. You were not kidding around.

I snatched your little person up and carried you into the front room because it was carpeted. I stood at the bay window and rocked you as you howled. 'Oh God, oh God,' I crooned as your cries ebbed from fright to rebuke to self-comfort, *mmm, mmm*. Outside, it was a beautiful winter morning, crisp and chill and clear. A woman pushed a double buggy through the pristine light, fully dressed, hair brushed, both children content, a third one at her heel on a scooter, and I wondered how the hell she managed it.

* * *

I pulled a hat onto your head. Concealing the bump on your forehead was my ulterior motive. You took the hat by the bobble and dropped it on the floor. Your ulterior motive was to thwart my ulterior motive. 'But it's cold outside, darling,' I cajoled in a sweet voice as I tried to get it back on. Just put the fucking thing on, we're late. The Baby and Toddler Group ran from nine thirty until eleven. It was already after ten. I had gotten breakfast into you, a more complicated process than it sounds. Changed you, dressed you – again: more complicated than it sounds. You did not want to be changed, you did not want to be dressed. I produced a shoe only to find you'd pulled off your sock. I put the sock back on while you pulled off the other one. I put that one back on while you pulled off the first. Oh, it was all so stupid. People think that looking after an infant is basic. I know this because I once thought so myself.

I gave up on the socks and looked at you. How committed you were to being a baby. You stayed up half the night practising. 'I can't do this,' I confessed. 'I'm so tired.'

You smiled. I flopped down on the rug beside you.

I may or may not have fallen asleep. You stuck your hand in my mouth.

The nappy bag. Soother, spare soother, nappies, wipes. 'This would all happen much faster if you weren't whining like that, darling,' I called in my eminently rational voice as I tracked down the various items. I used to do that sometimes, passive-aggressively address you as another adult to illustrate how reasonable I was and, by extension, how unreasonable you were. Barrier cream, burp cloth, change of clothes, Calpol. Blanket, bib, spare bib – 'honestly, we'd already be there if you just stopped making that awful sound and let me think' – tissues, phone, Sophie the Giraffe, coins for baby morning, keys. 'Okay, alright, I hear you. Jesus.'

When I returned with the packed nappy bag, you had vomited down your front. I saw the time on the clock and said a very bad word.

* * *

We made it out the door.

We made it out the door! You were yelling the word *Stuck* from the buggy. Or wait, that hadn't started yet. It was cute the first time.

We made it onto the street.

We made it onto the street!

44

A guard of honour of wheelie bins flanked its length, but not our wheelie bin. The bin lorry was at the top of the road working its way down. Handbrake turn.

* * *

I had recently switched your buggy seat from facing me to facing the world so I could no longer see your face, just your wispy hair. I put your hat back on. A hand reached up, pulled it off and tossed it overboard. I stopped the buggy, picked up the hat, put it back on your flossy head, set off. The hand reached up again and this time flung the hat. I unpicked it from the neighbour's hedge.

Inside the parish hall, the buggies were slotted together in the corridor like supermarket trolleys. I unstrapped my prize marrow and followed the noise to a room containing maybe ten other babies and toddlers, their mothers and minders seated along the walls. I set you down on the edge of the playmat and you motored straight to the heart of the action with not so much as a backward glance. I took a photo and shared it with my husband. *Socialised.* He sent back a smiley face.

I paid my few euro and was offered tea and a biscuit. Screams. I turned to see you with a car in your fist and another baby sitting on his bottom howling for it. I prised the car from your cold dead grip and returned it to the other baby. He stopped screaming but you started. Jesus, that sound. A quick-thinking woman held out a different car to you. 'Look at this cool red one!' You accepted the cool red one, which the other baby then cried for. 'Wow, that's some bump, little fella!' the woman remarked and the other baby pitched forward to peer at it.

Suddenly everyone was staring at my baby. 'Yeah. He walloped himself this morning.'

'It's supposed to be good when a bump pops up,' said the woman who had given me the tea. 'It's when they get a bang on the head and there's no bump that you have to worry.'

'Oh. Why?'

'Dunno. Something to do with the swelling being on the outside and not on the brain, maybe? Concussion?'

We all made *hmmm, interesting* sounds. At least when you could see the damage, you knew where you stood, right?

Another woman picked her baby up. 'The nurse told me to take my little man off his back because he was getting flat head syndrome. Look.' She turned him around. He had a head like a saucepan. More *hmmmm, interesting* sounds.

'You should have seen the state of her skull by the time she'd been squeezed through the birth canal,' said the mother of a little girl with a frilly pink garter on her head. 'She looked like an alien. They put her into my arms and I was like, oh Jesus, cone-head, but I was too freaked out to say anything to my husband, and he was too freaked out to say anything to me. It really damaged our first moments together.'

'They should tell you that stuff to prepare you. Why don't they tell women that stuff?'

'Would you have had a baby if they told you that stuff?' This was my contribution.

We paused to sniff the air.

'I think that's me,' said one of the women. She lifted her baby off the playmat, sniffed the nappy, then slung the child over her shoulder. No negotiating, no hysterics, no wrestling. No ear-shattering, outraged dirty protest. The woman was back in a minute or two – a minute or two! – with a fragrant infant whom she returned to the mat.

You were moving in on the girl with the frilly pink garter. I don't know, Sailor, but if you were a girl, I'd raise you the same as a boy for as long as we could get away with it. What you wouldn't do to me if I slapped a pink garter on your head. But the little girl tolerated it and that made me sad. For her, for the mother who put it on her, for our entire gender. How good we were, how biddable.

The little girl was putting a plastic yellow egg into a plastic blue egg box, then taking it back out. Putting it in. Taking it out. Entirely oblivious to the fact that you were creeping up on her. It was a wildlife documentary.

She clocked you and froze. You were upon her by then and reached out. The little girl clutched the egg to her chest. You stretched past the egg and went for the garter, tugged it from her head and frowned at it for a few seconds before tossing it away. *Go on, my son!* I wanted to cheer. *That's my boy!*

Then the women were all on their feet, the infancy infantry, stacking chairs, sorting toys, collecting cups. One washed dishes at the sink in the corner while another dried and put them away. I towered over the busy babies trying to look useful and, failing, picked you up. You screamed down the house as I bundled you out of there. Oh yes, Sailor, how you screamed.

* * *

The clouds were purple with impending rain so I hurried along. Some dick had parked half up on the footpath. The buggy got wedged between the car and the wall as the first fat raindrops fell. I reversed it out and waited for a gap in the traffic, then lowered you onto the road and scuttled around the car. It abruptly bucketed down and you squealed. I heaved the buggy back onto the kerb and went rummaging in the tray for the rain cover. There was an umbrella down there too. I opened the umbrella and clamped the handle between shoulder and ear like a phone while I fitted the clear plastic rain cover over your foot muff and scrabbled around for the knobs to hook the loops onto. You squealed again as a squall blew more rain in on you.

The loops didn't reach the knobs. The wretched thing was upside down. Oh, it was all so stupid. As I rotated the cover, a gust of wind snatched the umbrella away. I made a grab for it only for the buggy to roll towards the traffic. The driver of an oncoming car screeched to a halt as I lunged and caught the handle just before you were tipped onto the road. A trickling face stared out at me through the windscreen.

The shock. My heart hammered with it. You were bawling. The car remained stationary, the driver gaping out at the stupid woman who had almost killed her child. I reversed the buggy to safety and applied the brake, got the rain cover on.

Then I retrieved the upturned umbrella. The water that had accumulated in it doused my scalp, then the umbrella was whipped inside out.

The washing machine had ratcheted up to its final spin by the time I made it home. I detached the rain cover. Your eyes were shut. Nap time was my chance to work. Work! The membrane was thin that day. Between coping and not. I carried you upstairs, laid you down in the cot and stepped back. You are so beautiful when you're asleep.

* * *

I was in forced sunny-disposition mode when the automatic doors of the supermarket ushered us inside that afternoon. Which is part of the problem. All these women going around feigning jolliness to get their children to comply? You could be forgiven for thinking they are having actual fun. I had even remembered to bring a coin for the trolley but you wouldn't consent to sitting in it so I steered it with one hand while holding you to my hip with the other.

Involve your child in the preparation of their food, the fussy-eater book had said. 'Well, isn't that a lovely bunch of bananas? Yes it is!' Berries. I put in two punnets. Aspirational. 'How do you like them apples?' In went the tray. Talk to your child about their food, the book had advised. 'Check out this joker.' I wobbled a head of broccoli. '*Wubba wubba.*' You gurgled in delight. You wouldn't be gurgling in delight when it reappeared on your plate.

Next up, a grubby heap of root vegetables. 'Oh!' I remarked, 'roundy!' There wasn't much else to be said for them. Turnips, read the sign. Was it possible I had never encountered a turnip before? You watched as a big boy – and two years old qualified as a big boy to your mind – followed his mother with one of those plastic shopping baskets on wheels, the long handle over his head like a pony and trap. Although you could barely walk unaided, you decided that you too needed a wheelie basket, and thrashed about in my arms like a fish. I grabbed a basket, put you down, lowered the handle over your head and placed it into your hands to help you balance. Off you tottered after the boy. I took a photo and shared it with my husband. He sent back a smiley face.

I picked up a turnip. Purple blotched its buff face like a port wine stain. I turned it over in my hand, surprised by its heft. *Alas, poor Yorick, I knew him well.*

Holy shit, what is that?

It's a turnip, apparently. Medieval, huh? Would you believe: I've never held a turnip before.

Me neither. Do something new every day they say, right?

Right. That's what they say. Might take it bowling.

Dear friends, treasured friends, greatly missed. If they could see me now, that little gang of mine. Buying turnips.

That little gang of mine. I looked down, then around. Gone. You were not on the fruit and veg aisle. Nor on the bread aisle. I hurried into the random section. No sign. I double-backed to the entrance in case you'd wandered out and I pressed my palms against the glass. The automatic doors wouldn't open from that side.

I ran along the tops of the aisles calling your name. Hard to breathe. Detach my child and you detach my air supply. The umbilical cord is a two-way street.

A strangled whimper when I finally saw you. The pony and trap had overturned at the tins. An older woman was helping you out of the harness. Peppers were strewn across the floor, traffic-light colours. I hadn't put peppers in the basket. You howled when you saw me and raised your arms to be lifted.

'I looked away for a second,' I told the woman. 'I only looked away for a second.'

'He's grand,' the woman said, patting you down. 'Big strong boy like that. It was a bad bend, wasn't it, pet? Wasn't that all it was? A bad bend at too fast a clip. Ah sure you poor little fella, you came a cropper.' I took you into my arms and the woman collected the peppers while I told her to leave them, leave them, I'll do it, leave them.

'He didn't start crying until he saw you,' she confided when she straightened up. 'He's playing up to his mammy. They're divils for it, the boys. I have five of them.'

I carried you back to the trolley and this time you consented to be lowered into the fold-down seat. Judging by your face, we were on a clock. The time bomb was ticking down. 'Oh look at this yummy new breakfast cereal!' I wheedled as I scanned the box for the many, many different words for sugar. You objected to me touching the trolley handle, peeling my fingers off every time I tried to steer it. I nudged it along with my hip. The countdown to hysterics had commenced.

I moved through the aisles as briskly as I was able, which wasn't very briskly, which wasn't very able. The shopping list which had been in my hand before I lost you was nowhere to be found. 'Bouncy, bouncy bog roll, *boing*!' I exclaimed hopefully, trying to talk you down from the same ledge on which I found myself.

Another toddler in a trolley stared you down as his mother pushed him past. You stared coldly back. The child's face was a smeared five o'clock shadow of brown. In his fist was a chocolate cookie. Without taking his eyes off you, he returned the cookie to his mouth, took another bite and chewed slowly, deliberately – malevolently, I want to say. You turned to me and howled for the cookie and I judged the child's mother, yes, I dealt her a sound judging for making life harder for the good mothers who provided healthy snacks. The ones who mislaid their children in supermarkets.

'Here, look at these!' I said with brittle brightness, offering my coveted set of car keys.

'Dah!' you instructed me imperiously, your hand outstretched toward the cookie. 'Dah! Dah!'

'Wow, what is this!' I gasped, dangling the metal insert that unlocked the trolley from the one in front, but you were having none of it.

'DAH!'

'*Vroom, vroom?*' I tried, swerving the trolley from side to side, but the game was up. You opened your mouth and let loose.

It was supermarket sweep after that, grabbing whatever

I could remember to grab while you screamed and tried to clamber out of the seat. The check-out queues were long. Only two tills were open. Then a third opening was announced and I dashed across. A man appeared from backstage and sat behind the register.

Milk and nappies, milk and nappies – I checked and rechecked the two items I always ran out of but couldn't remember anything else from the list. Wipes! It was too late to run back: the till operator had already started checking my groceries through and a line had formed behind me. You whined and you grizzled and you bawled in my face – the stress. It was all so stupid. My life was all so stupid.

By the time I had unloaded everything onto the conveyor belt, the packing dock was jammed. The cashier had stacked my purchases in a mound, like the heap of turnips. The heavy items which I had placed on the belt first so that I could pack them at the bottom of the shopping bags were buried beneath the lighter, more delicate things – the eggs and bananas and all those peppers that I really didn't want.

When I tried to unearth the milk cartons and tins, the items on top came slithering down. The cashier was moving faster than I could, firing products through with a *bip, bip* like it was a video game. My face burned with the awareness of the queue backing up behind me and my embarrassment was the most embarrassing thing of all. Grown woman! I shovelled my purchases into the shopping bags any which way.

The cashier perched the two megapacks of nappies on top of everything and told me how much I owed. As I searched my pockets, one of the megapacks slid off. I made a grab for it and dropped my phone.

And the thing is, Sailor, he had no idea. To him I was yet another clumsy housewife who couldn't keep up with him. I know this because I used to think that way too. I used to be a dick. There's a spectrum. I was on it. But you won't be a dick because I have enlightened you. Be an astronaut, be a nurse, be a postman, be whatever. Just don't be a dick.

The screen on my phone hadn't shattered. I held it to the card reader and waited for the *ding*. My purchases weren't fully packed up.

The assistant handed me my receipt then started firing the next woman's groceries onto mine so now I was holding her up. Last to be turfed into the bag was old Yorick, bursting one of the peppers. Alas.

* * *

I opened my eyes. Living-room chair. I may or may not have been asleep. You were driving a car around my feet. Dusk. Finishing line in sight.

The turnip had a face only a mother could love. I held it steady and pushed down the knife but made little impression on the flesh. You started griping in your high chair, bored already with your Play-Doh. I put down the knife and cleaned the Play-Doh off your tray, separating the colours into the right tubs before they dried out. I set you up with kinetic sand to buy myself another ten minutes. I hated kinetic sand. It got everywhere. 'Oh Jesus,' I sighed when I saw the time. I was behind, so behind. And so tired.

Back to the chopping board. This called for the man knife. I unsheathed it from my husband's Japanese steel knife block and tingled inside. There is a piece of gristle, a rubbery nugget secreted away in my pelvis that I was unaware of until you arrived. You must have flicked a switch as you exited my uterus because it began transmitting around about then. When you had banged your head against the tiles that morning, I had felt it in my groin. And it is alert to knives, this squeamish article, which may – now that I think about it – be that arch expander and contracter, my cervix, wincing away. Do not be afraid of these female parts, Sailor. Be aware, be not afraid, be not a dick.

The weight of that knife. Men and their superior toys. I applied the blade hard. The squeamish component didn't like that but the knife descended and sliced off a third of the turnip.

You started to whine. 'That was not ten minutes,' I told you as I picked at the seam of a roll of cling film. 'That was not even five minutes.' Hated cling film. Hated it more than I hated kinetic sand. Defeated by something that lacked a third dimension. While I'd been off tinkering on the cerebral plane, the smart money had been mastering its dark art. If you don't keep up with technology, it bypasses you, Sailor, but if you don't keep up with its opposite, the manual realm, it bypasses you just as surely and suddenly there you are, a creature overtaken by evolution, obsolete, baying at the shoreline. 'Wah!' you protested from the high chair. 'Wah!'

I parked the cling film and instead put the leftover turnip cut side down on a plate. 'Alright, coming.' I swiped as much of the kinetic sand as I could back into the tub and substituted it with Duplo bricks and a dinosaur. Then put the turnip into the fridge and took out the bag of meat.

I picked up the knife and got the tingling feeling again. Sometimes when a train approaches you get an impulse to jump. Everyone experiences this, you will too, it's nothing to worry about, just your imagination flexing itself, exploring the potential extremities of life and, in considering your condition from a radical perspective, realising yourself more fully, kind of like you do now when pretending to be Superman. When I picked up that knife, the tingling reminded me of your vulnerability. Protect him, my imagination was exhorting me: he would be so easy to kill. That dream I had of you. Your shoulders no broader than a cereal box but I had to sever your spine and you were so good about it, smiling at me as you held my leg to keep yourself upright, trusting that I knew what I was doing when, oh God, I did not.

The real you, perched on high, banged your Duplo like a gavel and screeched. Your cries sometimes felt physical, jabs of a stick. I jumped to them, your dancing bear. The bears are not dancing, Sailor. That is not dancing. I set down the knife and released you. You signalled with a swimming motion your desire to get at the open cupboard. I placed you in front of the tins.

The butcher had already sliced the meat. He'd held up a slab for my approval and I'd said yes like I knew what I was doing. 'Is it for a casserole, love?' he enquired and, thinking this was a bit of professional banter, that a degree of role-play was expected here, me as the mammy and him as the cheeky chappie who understands her need to produce something for her husband's tea, I nodded, because it is a part you have to learn to play, the mother. You don't automatically know how to talk to the butchers and bakers and candlestick makers who treat you so differently once you push a pram through their door. A public-health nurse – several health professionals, in fact – called me Mum or Mam long before you could. Could you take his pram suit off for me there, please, Mam? Could you place him on the scales for me there, please, Mum? How is that not weird? Now here I was, the lapsed vegetarian, in a butcher's of all places, with a buggy of all things, buying half a pound of flesh I didn't want. I glanced around the shop. Were we all wondering how it had come to this?

The butcher slapped the meat onto his block and set about removing the thick rind of fat, but then he sliced the rest of the slab into bite-sized pieces. *Stop!* I wanted to blurt. 'Thanks,' I said instead. Now I would have to go through every individual segment looking for those thin elasticky strips. It would have been so much easier to chase them down were the steak intact.

I emptied the bag of meat onto the chopping board. It was cold and slimy. I spliced away at the sinewy tissue like a surgeon removing a cancer, knowing I was getting too per-fectionist about it, knowing I was against the clock. But it was for you. If stringy meat found its way into your mouth, the meal would be over. You were so skinny and pale back then, the thin white duke. 'How old is he?' one of the playgroup mothers had asked me that morning, and then, 'Oh,' when we established you were older than her significantly larger child.

I cried over the onions and chopped the carrots. I cannot be the first woman to wonder how many vegetables I have peeled. That figure should be displayed on our gravestones: *This woman peeled however many tonnes of potatoes, let's hear it for Mrs Whatever!* And her husband? Well, he just ate them.

You had stacked the tins on top of one another to form a pyramid. That was a new development. Took a photo, shared it with my husband. He sent back a smiley face.

The vegetable peeler was not up to the job of removing the skin from the turnip. I lowered it with a sigh. Oh, it was all so stupid. So manual and relentless and stupid. Trimming the meat had knocked me off schedule. At least it was dark. At least the day was coming to an end. Then I could go back to bed. It was all about killing the days when you were small, getting them over and done with. Before you were born, it was all about living them. Achieving, advancing – stuff like that. I pushed aside the chopping board to make room for the spice tin, accidentally tipping the man knife over the edge where you were playing . . .

I lunged and caught it.

I couldn't look down. I could not look down at your busy little person, pootling away with the tins. I dropped the knife into the sink like a murder weapon. I could hardly cry because

I could hardly breathe, I was just this slumped *thing* holding onto the neck of the tap with one hand, the other turning the stream of water red. The filthiest words started to spill out of me. Low and guttural, they spewed down the plughole with the watery blood.

When I finally looked down, you weren't even there. You had crossed over to the other side of the room to pull the bottom shelf of books out of the bookcase.

'Fuck you,' I growled down the phone at my husband, my hand wrapped in a tea towel. My voice was hoarse from my earlier imprecations. I didn't know myself. I did not know this woman. 'Fuck you for packing away my normal knives when you moved in with me. Fuck you for buying these Japanese ones that cost a hundred quid each and will slice through anything because you deserve the best but you *never fucking use them* because you *never fucking cook*. Fuck you for what you have done to my life.'

'What are you talking about?' my husband was saying calmly. 'I don't know what you're talking about. I am in the office. I can't discuss this right now. We can discuss this when I get home.'

Over by the bookcase, a small frightened face was blinking at me. I hung up and sat on the floor beside you and took you onto my lap. We rootled into each other as we rocked. Loving you was the easy part. Loving you was the only easy part. Your flossy hair and the bump on your forehead and the wonderful heat of your skin, the wonderful alive heat. *Hush little Darling, don't say a word.* Couldn't remember the next line so I sang that one a few more times. The day you were born a door appeared – or was revealed, really, having been there all along – the door out of life, the door when it's over, you're done, *thank you: next*, and I have to go through it first. Are you listening to me? Do not go through that door before me. This is the natural order, Sailor. Do not rupture the natural order. Or I'll kill you, I'll kill myself.

* * *

I had just put rice on the hob when I got the smell. You kicked off when I grabbed you from the playmat to cart you upstairs to the change table. 'Now then,' I said over your fury, 'let's get you all cleaned up.'

'No,' I protested as your hand descended into the soiled nappy. I plucked a wipe and removed the poo from your fingers as best I could, then bandaged it in a second wipe until I could get you to the sink. By which time, you'd moved your bottom out of the nappy. The poo was now up your back and on the changing mat. 'Stop!' I commanded when you decided to get up. A potato print of poo had mysteriously appeared on your tummy. I twisted my arm to look at the side of my hand. A wet brown smear. There were not enough wipes. Now I'd have to bathe you. Down in the kitchen, my phone was ringing. 'Shut up!' I shouted at it.

What is it about bathing a baby? Of the many moments of loveliness this life offers, it's right up there. You were splashing in the bath when an alarm went off. I grabbed your wet body and raced downstairs into acrid smoke. The rice. I'd left the hob on full to bring it to the boil. I jabbed the handle of the sweeping brush at the ceiling-mounted smoke alarm while you screamed at a similar pitch, but I wasn't able to make the connection. Then you couldn't scream for coughing. So I opened the back door and left the smoking pot on the step for someone to trip over later, threw open the windows to the cold night air and ran with my wet coughing baby back upstairs. Then downstairs once more because we couldn't listen to that alarm one second longer, could we, Sailor? I deposited you naked and bawling on the playmat, stood on a chair and pressed the red button. The room was so smoky that the alarm came straight back on again so I knocked the batteries out. And finally upstairs into the lovely warm bath to wash my bloody handprints off your shivering skin.

* * *

A text as I was putting the dinner out in the cold and sour-smelling kitchen. *Something has come up here. Eat without me. X.* I had missed two calls from him.

'Good boy, well done,' I said, trying to fool you into thinking you had already complied with my efforts to insert you into the high chair. 'That's it, good job,' while I tilted your body to angle a leg in. It was like threading a needle, where the thread has agency and hates needles. 'Hey look, a dog!' I exclaimed at the window, though it was dark out. You twisted around and I got your left then right leg into the slots in quick succession. 'Oh, the dog has just gone.' Thunder face. 'It was cute,' I offered, when you realised you were in stocks. You tore off your bib and cast it to the floor like a man quitting his job.

'What sound does a dog make?' I lined your high chair up with the dining table. Eat family meals together, the fussy-eater book had said.

'Woof,' you conceded.

'What sound does a duck make?'

'Quack.' Warming to the topic.

'What sound does a horse make?'

'Neigh.'

I opened the puppy book that made the barking sounds and recited the first rhyme while extending a spoon of mush your way. 'Open up,' I said. 'That's it!' though it wasn't – you were studying the puppies with a pursed mouth. I realised my own mouth was agape in encouragement. Looking stupid again – I shut it. 'Be the little puppy getting his dinner. Here little puppy, open wide.' You opened your mouth and I got the spoon in. Goal. I recited the next rhyme by way of reward.

'Restrict the milk,' the public-health nurse had advised me as she frowned at the graph charting your descent down the centiles, a word that didn't exist in my day. 'It will encourage him to accept solids,' she explained. 'Yeah,' my husband told me when I reported this information back to him, as if he were reporting it to me. 'He's not hungry. If he's not hungry, he won't eat.' He didn't understand, nobody understood, least of all me.

'Here, cutie puppy! Come here, boy!' Coaxing a wild animal to eat from my palm. The shy fawn was considering it. Any moment now, he would place his silken muzzle in my hand. He would eat and he would thrive. If the fawn didn't thrive, I didn't thrive. That was our ecosystem.

I moved the spoon an inch closer. Three teaspoons and you would survive. Four and we were into bonus time. 'Best little puppy.' Another inch closer again.

You averted your face.

Your sleeve is in your dinner, my husband remarked. He wasn't there but he didn't have to be there. He was always there when things were going wrong. Yet never there to help. The luxury, the sheer luxury of sending a last-minute message saying you wouldn't be home that evening. It would be a decade – more – before I could do the same. *What does he eat?* he had texted me the one time he was left in charge.

I pushed my plate out of the way and offered the teaspoon again. *Two playful little puppies, Jess and Jake are their names. They want to go outside, and play their favourite games.* You pushed the barking button. *Yap, yap, yap.* Your mouth opened up. The spoon went in. Mental victory dance. 'Who's the best little puppy!' Two down, one to go.

The teaspoon made another approach. This time you batted it away, flicking orange mush across the wall. 'Jesus!' I had snapped before I could stop myself. You burst into tears, the sound of woodland hooves taking flight. I put the spoon on the plate and my head in my hands. I was so tired. I was so tired and you were so hungry. But you wouldn't eat and I couldn't sleep. Mother and child.

* * *

'Everything okay?'

My husband used to answer the phone to me with *Hey*, pronouncing it in such a way I could hear he was smiling.

'He won't eat,' I said in that tight voice I hate. Same thing I said every night.

'Restrict the milk.' Same thing he said.

'He hasn't had a bottle since lunchtime.'

'Why did you give him a bottle at lunchtime?'

'Because he wouldn't eat lunch.'

'He won't eat because you're giving him too many bottles. He's not hungry.'

'He is hungry. And dehydrated. He barely ate *breakfast*.' Shrill voice, the one I hated even more.

'You need to calm down. He won't eat because you're stressing him out.' He won't eat because you, because you, because you. It was so easy for him behind his desk. He hadn't lain on his side that morning extending bits of toast under the table where you were playing. You had chewed the first buttered soldier and inserted the second into the cabin of your fire engine.

In the background, you were howling for your bottle. 'Thanks for pointing out that it's all my fault,' I told him. 'That's a great help.'

'You're shouting at me again,' he observed with infuriating composure, although I wasn't shouting: I was making myself heard over your racket. I responded with a curse.

'Don't curse in front of our child,' he instructed me, so I responded with another one and hung up.

Back to the dining table. I slumped beside you and your sobs subsided from furious to forlorn. We looked at each other and I stroked your hair, ran my thumb over the contour of the bump, already turning purple. Ashamed of myself for fighting in front of you, ashamed for cursing. Ripping the colourful screen of your child's world, revealing the ugliness of the adult world behind it. Outside it was lashing. That burnt pot. It was going to take forever to clean. 'Mama left the rice out in the rain,' I sang to you. 'I don't think that I can take it. Because it took so long to make it. And I'll never have that recipe again. Oh no!' I struggled on the high note and smiled. You smiled back. 'Please eat?' I asked hopefully and pushed the button on the puppy book. *Yap, yap, yap.* 'Be the hungry little puppy. Just one more bite and you can have your bottle.' But the forest fawn had long since bolted. I unshackled you from the high chair.

* * *

My baby was crying in hunger. I could not feed my baby. It was your bottle you wanted. And only your bottle. The entirety of your being was focused on that want, that need in your life. The entirety of my being was focused on the want, the need, to nourish you. I offered you water. You drank a little and turned it into tears. Around and around the house we went, your head on my shoulder, bawling in my ear, me singing in yours. *The wheels on the bus go round and round.* Returning to the kitchen every third or fourth circuit to produce a morsel from the fridge or cupboard. Bits of banana,

65

crackers, yogurt. Rejected. I ate them myself. *Round and round, round and round.* 'Toddler won't eat,' I googled over your shoulder for the millionth time. Your weight in my arms was no weight at all.

It was late, well past your bedtime, when I finally gave up and gave in and gave you your bottle, followed by a second one. You gulped them between sobs and passed out in my arms.

* * *

I may or may not have been asleep when my husband came home. I raised my head from the kitchen table at the sound of his key in the door. The counters were clean. The knife was back in the knife block. Orange mush no longer spattered the wall. *Thwump, thwump* went the dishwasher, chugging away, *round and round.* I loved that dishwasher. It was the only one that helped me.

My husband took in this scene of domestic order then sniffed the air. 'What's that smell?'

It was a reasonable question.

'I burnt the rice.'

'How can you burn rice?'

Again, a reasonable question, or would have been, pre-motherhood. How can you do anything right? was the question now. With so many obstacles strewn in your path? So many chaotic variables? But I was just a stupid housewife who couldn't even boil rice. Twenty minutes it had taken to get that pot clean, the grains like small black insects welded to the base. I had soaked, I had scrubbed, I had scoured.

66

'I burnt it, okay? I burnt the rice. But you ruined my life. So we're quits.'

'Okaaay,' he said. 'Do you want to talk about it?'

I sighed. Too much to explain, too tired to explain it. He sat down and I stood up, opened the fridge. The decapitated head of the turnip. I moved my husband's dinner to the microwave then the table. *Schlep, schlep, round and round.* Cutlery, glass of water.

He frowned at the plate. 'Why were you making rice for stew?'

'It's a casserole. He won't eat potatoes. Plus it's brown rice. Wholegrains.'

Upstairs, you cried. I waited to see whether my husband would offer to go. 'This is delicious,' he said instead, though it wasn't: it was healthy. 'Leave him, he'll fall back asleep,' he called when I was halfway up the stairs to establish that it wasn't him shirking duty but me being overzealous.

When I came back downstairs ten or so minutes later, knowing you still weren't fully asleep and that I'd be up and down those stairs several more times before the night was out, your father was in the front room watching *Blade Runner* again. He looked up and smiled at me sweetly. 'I love you,' he said. The curtains were open. How homely we must have looked from the outside, the husband on the recliner smiling lovingly up at his wife. I love you because you do everything, he was telling me, even though you are exhausted, your eyes hollow sockets. I love you because you haven't had a day off in over a year now yet still you keep going, slogging on in sickness and in health, raising our child so I don't have to. I love you and will tell you so to deflect your criticism and assuage my guilt.

I sat on the couch. 'How was your day?' I asked him and he embarked on tales of valour and derring-do from a distant galaxy. Things he had said, problems he had solved, names, many names, people I would never meet. It was too tiring to try to imagine them.

'You're not listening.'

I opened my eyes. May or may not have been asleep. 'Sorry. How was your day?'

'I just told you.'

'Oh. You did. Sorry.'

'How was *your* day?'

'My day?' I wondered, drawing a blank. Nothing recorded. Vegetative state. 'Em,' I said, 'long.' Then I remembered the supermarket and wanted to tell him about the young fella who fired my groceries down the chute at me like I was target practice and how flustered I got when I couldn't keep up, but I realised how stupid that would make me look, that that's all I had to say for myself. 'He didn't eat much for dinner.'

'And the Baby and Toddler Group?'

'Oh yeah. I dunno. He kept taking toys from the other babies and they'd cry, so I kept having to prise the toys out of his hands to return them, then he'd cry because he didn't understand that they weren't his toys so he spent most of the time crying. I don't know if I'll bring him again.'

'It's good for him to get used to other kids,' he pronounced. 'Good for you both to get out. Meet new people.'

'Mmm,' I murmured without conviction. I didn't want to meet new people. I wanted to meet my old people again.

'Did you get any work done?' Then 'What?' he protested when I flashed him a filthy look.

'Do you think I'm sitting around all day eating biscuits with other women?'

'When did I say that? I never said that.'

'You didn't have to.'

'Okay,' he said carefully. 'So when are we going to talk about your hand?'

I considered my palm. A blood-soaked wad of bog roll was strapped to it with Mickey Mouse plasters. 'I cut it,' I said. 'On your stupid giant knife.'

'Did you get it looked at?'

'How?' I nodded at your end of the ceiling. 'How can I go to the doctor?'

'Just bring him with you.'

'Just!' I laughed. '*Just!*' I laughed again. 'You know how hard it is to battle him into a car and back out again at the best of times, then back in again, then back out again on the other end. I can't do that with an injured hand. Actually, you don't know, do you? You've never had to do it.'

'Why were you using my chef's knife? You hate my knives. You're always complaining about them.'

'Am I not allowed to use your knives now?'

'I'm just worried.'

69

'About what?'

'About the whole knives thing.'

'What whole knives thing?'

He switched *Blade Runner* off, got up from the recliner and took my bandaged hand. 'I was talking to' – another office name that meant nothing to me – 'and his wife's postnatal depression got so bad that she asked him to remove all the knives because she was scared she was going to harm herself.'

I took my hand back. 'This isn't postnatal depression.'

He raised his eyebrows sceptically.

'This is life-is-shit depression. All I do is housework and childcare and I'm sleep-deprived and think-deprived because I never get a moment to myself, not even in the toilet. I miss my old life like I'd miss a lover. I pine for it, I daydream about leaving you so that I can be with it again. You'd like to diagnose postnatal depression because then it's not your fault. Wait, you were discussing me in the office?'

'I was worried about you after that phone call.'

'Why didn't you rush home then?'

'I had a meeting.'

'You couldn't have been that worried, so.'

He pointed at his phone. 'One minute it's like an Instagram feed of our kid looking cute, the next you're screaming about knives like a madwoman, and then I come home to find you've harmed yourself.'

'I haven't *harmed* myself. It was an accident. If I was going to *harm* myself, I wouldn't start with my palm. How stupid do you think I am?

70

'No really,' I insisted when he lowered his head, 'how stupid do you think I am?'

'I think you are one of the most intelligent people I know.'

'No, you don't. You think I'm stupid. But you know what? If I didn't look stupid in that stupid supermarket, there wouldn't be healthy food on the stupid table. Not that he' – I pointed at the ceiling beneath your cot – 'even eats. If I didn't look stupid, he'd be parked in front of the TV for several hours a day while I got some work done but then who'd be stupid? Him. Studies show that screens before the age of two impact on a child's development. And he'd be fed crap out of pouches that had *organic* emblazoned across them to insult my alleged intelligence because if something has been heat-processed to that degree, who cares whether it's organic or not? So somebody has to look stupid. But why does it always have to be me?'

'I don't want to fight with you.'

'And I don't want to be this person,' I told him, and left the room to go to bed.

* * *

I was asleep when my husband came into the bedroom and switched on the light. 'What happened to his forehead?' he asked as I floundered about.

The unkindness of waking me. I shielded my eyes to gape up at him. Now? You decide to show interest in your child now? When I'm finally asleep? 'I told you on the phone. He banged it off the kitchen floor.'

71

'He fell?'

'No, he did it on purpose. I already told you this.'

'What do you mean?'

'I mean he did it on purpose. He raised his head' – I sat up in the bed and demonstrated with my own head – 'then walloped it off the kitchen floor.'

'What do you mean, he did it on purpose?'

'I mean he walloped his head off the floor on purpose. He just' – and I tilted my head back then jerked it forward a second time – 'walloped it.' Why was I showing my husband again? Stupid.

'What did the doctor say?'

'I didn't go to the doctor. You know I didn't go to the doctor. Why are you asking me something you already know?'

'Have you *seen* the size of the bump on his forehead?'

'Yes, I have *seen* the size of the bump on his forehead. I have been home with him all day.'

'I don't understand why you didn't bring him to the doctor, that's all.' He used to do that all the time, swoop in like the senior consultant to pass judgement on his junior doctor, whom he always found wanting.

'Look, if the level of care I am giving our son is unsatisfactory, feel free to step in. Feel free to do a whole ten minutes of parenting. Don't let me stop you.'

By this point, we were both standing over your sleeping body in the cot. Your father, the Professor of Paediatrics, was down on his hunkers examining the bump in relief. 'I still don't know what you mean by *he just did it*?'

'I mean he just did it. He just went *bang*. It sounded like a melon hitting the ground.'

'Christ. Why would he do that?'

'I don't know.'

'Was something going on?'

'I'd put him down on his playmat so I could get breakfast ready.'

'You said he did it on the tiles.'

'He crawled off the playmat to hit his head on the tiles. Are you actually trying to pick holes in my story?'

'So you put him down and then what?'

'*Nothing.* Well, I yelled at him.'

'You yelled at him?'

'He was whining his head off because I wasn't giving him my undivided attention and he'd already pulled out a lump of my hair and I'd had enough so I yelled.'

'Was this before or after you screamed at me about the knife?'

'The knife was dinner. He banged his head at breakfast.'

'You know you could be heard, don't you? You know people looked up and I had to leave the office and go out on the corridor because there was this hysterical screeching coming out of the phone.'

'I'm so sorry for embarrassing you.'

'Look,' he said, changing tack, 'I know how hard it is to be left alone all day with a child.'

'You don't know. How would you? You've never done it.'

'Well, I can imagine. I can imagine it would drive you insane.'

'Insane?'

He sighed.

'What are you saying to me?'

He sighed again.

'No really: what are you saying to me?'

'Just that it's hard. Being locked up all day with a baby. It'd drive anyone crazy.'

'Crazy?'

'You know what I mean.'

I took a step back. 'Oh my God, it crossed your mind that I did this?' I pointed at your sleeping body. 'It crossed your mind that I went *crazy* and banged our baby's head?'

He winced at these words and reached for my arm. 'That's not what I said.'

I took another step back. 'It did, though, didn't it? It crossed your mind.' I waited for him to deny it. To say: of course not! To declare that he could see my devotion to our child. I think I was actually fishing for compliments, God help me. I think I was actually expecting praise for working harder than I had ever worked in my life and for no material benefit to myself. To my material detriment, in fact.

'I didn't say that,' was all he managed.

'It entered your mind, fleetingly or otherwise, that I could lose control and hurt our little boy,' I summarised flatly, a statement not a question.

My husband stood still in your nursery, a backdrop of Winnie-the-Pooh wallpaper, forest-animal curtains, a light fitting shaped like the sun. Our attempt at a happy home.

'I love you,' he told me sadly.

A lurch as the dynamics of our marriage shifted underfoot. From the toybox came the sound of your jumbo jet taking off. The impulse to shove my husband hard in the chest was so strong that I turned and staggered away to thwart it, grappling with the doors and banisters that came rearing up at me as if on a conveyor belt because I wasn't in my right mind any more. I was firmly in my wrong mind and liable to do anything, so off I went, down the stairs, out the door, up the drive, through the gate, along the road, overcome by a wildness that I needed to convert to movement or else risk doing something stupid, and by stupid I mean destructive because words have many meanings, Sailor, and you must deploy them with care because they can inflict real hurt.

'Oh!' I said in surprise to the cold night air, finding the transition to outdoors entirely radical. They say a mother forgets the pain of giving birth but that is not my experience. It's everything outside of that pain that she forgets, everything that is not her child. In short: the rest of the world. But 'oh!' here it was. I had been shovelling coal in the bowels of the ship for so long that I had forgotten it even was a ship. It was one big furnace that I had to keep stoking or else we'd run aground. Until: a deck and an array of stars, the glittering ocean. My husband's quarters.

'You think that's in me?' I was still having the conversation as I blundered up the road in my slippers, still waiting for my husband to deny it – *How could I ever think you capable of such a thing!* – gasping the chill air and wiping away tears. The thought of anyone hurting your defence-less body was obscene beyond my ability to contemplate it, but that the perpetrator should be me? 'Me?' I heard myself exclaiming in disbelief. '*Me!*' Who would kill for you. Kill others, kill myself. I turned around, half expecting to see my husband coming down the street to kiss and make up, but those days were over.

I laughed. I cried. *Round and round.* I always knew that, as the mother, I would get the blame for everything. If you grow up to be a serial killer, if you stash decapitated heads in your fridge like half-eaten turnips, they will say it was the mother's fault. What I did not know was that the blame would start so soon. You cannot leave suspicions of such gravity hanging between you and the person you love – okay, Sailor? Suspicions are chisels. They cause cracks in the surface. Water gets in and the water turns to ice and splits people apart because water expands when it freezes and – Christ, it's going to take so long to explain life to you and even then, when I get to the end, it won't make any sense. A rupture of continental proportions had taken place between your father and me. They'll teach you one day in geography about plate tectonics. Earthquakes splitting land masses apart, oceans gushing into the void. I find the sea frightening and so should you. Unfathomable creatures mutating in the depths, adapting to darkness, coldness, crushing pressure; an environment hostile to life, or to our kind of life. I did not want to trawl its depths. You'll have grasped the general idea. Caught the drift, I was going to say, the continental drift that was under way between your father and me.

'And if I am, God help me,' (for was that not a scenario deserving of pity, a mother harming her baby?) 'capable of hurting our child' – the argument continued – 'shouldn't you get me some help?'

'Why can't *you* help?' it further dawned on me and it was a revelation. I turned around again but he was nowhere to be seen. If I was *going crazy* and *insane*, a *madwoman* locked up with a small child all day, and he was *so worried*, why couldn't he lighten the load by mucking in? Take you some week-end morning so I could sleep, put you to bed some weekend night so I could sleep. Why was I the one who had to be up and down all night, cleaning up after everyone, cleaning up before everyone – be in a constant state of cleaning up before and after people who untidied faster than I could tidy – be wrong, always wrong, always forgetting stuff, losing stuff, late. I would have offloaded all this down the phone only I had forgotten the bloody thing. 'He's your child too,' I would have pointed out. 'He has a father.' Yeah. Why couldn't I have a day off and go to work? Take a shower, pick an outfit, put on make-up, look good, Hugo Boss, office, status, a door I could shut. Be alone. Alone! Bliss. Knock off, pay cheque, dinner, *Blade Runner*, reclining seat. My husband's working life had not imploded with your arrival. It had, in fact, improved. Meals cooked, laundry done, home cleaned. It'd cost him if he had to pay for all that. Same as it had cost me. Sailor, you spend half your day telling me that everything is *so unfair* but seriously: you have no idea.

A car drove past and I saw what they saw: a lone woman out late at night in her pyjamas muttering away to herself. I ducked around a corner. *Look, Mama's going round the bend!* I wanted to tell you, but oh, oh. What struck me as the starkest contradiction of all was that, having navigated this much of life – the volatility of youth, of love and loss, the agony and the ecstasy – the closest I had come to losing my mind was during the period known as settling down.

Maybe it was the rush of cold air, or the liberation of being unhitched from the buggy, but I was fairly bounding along in my slippers, *schlepity schlepity*. My body was no longer fit. It was the body of a wife and mother, an indoor creature indentured to domesticity, a frilly pink garter on her head. Tethered to duty but not anchored by it. I cast off the garter and broke into a run. I ran as if I had an assignation, as if I would meet my self at the end of the road, the old me, the real me, find her waiting on the corner. I would tell her that she was free. She had not known about her freedom. Only in losing it did she understand what she had lost.

I reached the end of the road. No one was waiting for me there.

The day after I got you home from the hospital, or the day after that – they blended together, the blurred days and the blurred nights, dark matter to be trudged through, all the blood I had lost – I sat at the kitchen table contemplating a bleak vista through the window. A fine drizzle was falling. Or maybe it wasn't: when I blinked, it seemed to clear. I was recovering from surgery. No, I was not recovering. Recovery requires rest. There was too much to be done to sleep or eat. Or even go to the toilet. New mothers say this in amazement, laughing like it's funny, when it's not funny, and we're not laughing: we're bewildered, we are floored. Our laughter is the public face of our incredulity. We can't even go to the toilet, ha ha! The starkness of the path ahead was revealed as the hormones flooded out of me, a phenomenon they call the baby blues though they are not blue. They are not any colour. They are the colour draining from your world.

There was less of you the day the public-health nurse showed up than there had been the day you were born. 'Might be time to supplement with formula?' she suggested as she packed away her scales. 'But I don't want him to get hooked,' I blurted, as if formula were an addiction and breast-milk the cure. My newborn was struggling. He was failing to thrive. It was the lowest point in my life. Soon to be followed by a lower point. And a lower one again.

And you know, men, men, *men* nod solemnly at that *Blade Runner* speech – tears in rain and fires on Orion – and they feel themselves part of a noble endeavour, believe they've experienced something epic right there with a beer on the couch. Here's my ennobling truth, Sailor: women risk death to give life to their babies. They endure excruciating pain, their inner parts torn, then they pick themselves up no matter what state they are in, no matter how much blood they've lost, and they tend to their infants. Your fires on Orion and your Luke, I am your father. Tell me, men: when were you last split open from the inside?

The seas are deep, Sailor, and the seas are dark. I have shown you the glittering surface. That is all you need to know. You can get by quite contentedly on this green Earth without ever plumbing its depths. The glittering surface is in no way representative of what lurks beneath. There are creatures down there, weird ugly species, and we have survived the millennia without knowing of their existence. They might survive too if they don't encounter ours. If we look, we will find them, and then we will know them. What knowledge will they bring us? Only how life forms contort. Did I need to know my husband was capable of harbouring such suspicions about me? Did he need to know? Better had that information remained in its watery grave.

The hormones running out of me and with them the colour. In my arms this scrap, this finely wrought scrap with long limbs and fingers delicate as wings but no inclination to feed, and it was grim and it was real, not some far-fetched story about androids set to an orchestral score to render my screen time meaningful, for there is nothing more meaningful than bringing a life into this world and fighting to keep it alive. From the outside a woman cradling a newborn looks peaceful. A new mother is not peaceful but in a jittery state of high alert. We declare her serene so we can leave her to it. So we can behold the glittering surface, remark on its beauty, and walk away.

Oh angry, Sailor. An angry woman. Shovelling coal all day in the bowels of the ship, my indenture ship. I butted my slippered toe on an uneven paving slab and howled louder than the pain justified. I howled like a wolf. A loury grey wolf; sharp teeth, bristly pelt. It felt good.

* * *

I had loved him. And he had loved me. That's what passed through my mind as I looked through the window at my husband's face in the blue light of the television screen. Our love was a song, I thought. I couldn't quite remember how the song went but I couldn't quite forget it either. Phrases of melody kept drifting past. I strained to catch them but in straining, lost them.

How small our house looked from the outside, yet how much it contained. A world, your world. Another lie. This was the world out here: vast, restless, dangerous – like my rage, Sailor, my escalating rage, which would no longer fit inside our home. I was at large now with the roaming pack of wolves who would huff and would puff and would blow the house down. Husband, I bayed at the bay window, you thought wolves were extinct in this land? I thought so too. The sea is not glittering and the mothers are not serene and the wolves were never more alive than they are tonight. They are volatile, they are vengeful, and you have summoned them to your door.

A bird shrieked, the noise piercing on the cold air. The week before, I had come upon a beak in the garden, a shred of purple sinew still attached. It was wide open in a screech, a small yellow hinge, and I'd hooked it onto a stick and flicked it into the bin before you found it, though perhaps I should expose you to life's cruelties. Perhaps I should prepare you. I was unprepared myself. Look how that worked out. Birds do not sleep in nests at this time of year. There's a fact that took me by surprise. Birds are not tucked up together in little feathered nests at night. They perch where they can, under hedges, eaves, shrubs. Many die of the cold. They don't teach you this stuff in school. In the morning, the birds sing. They *sing*. Can this really be song? Or yet another lie we tell ourselves? Are the birds like mothers in sunny-disposition mode? Simply trying to get through the day? Their bright demeanour does not mean the mothers are happy. Or even coping. It means that they are trying. They are doing their best. Snapping those frilly pink garters onto their heads and getting on with the job because somebody must. That is all it means. That and, of course, their love.

The bird shrieked again. The sweat on my skin had turned cold and I shivered. There was a lot to be said for a nest.

You cried. I heard it from outside. Clear as a bell.

Silence as you drifted back to sleep. Dreamed your dreams.

Then proper crying. Awake crying. Get-out-of-bed-and-pick-you-up crying. I waited for your father to comfort you. I counted while I waited. *Nineteen, twenty.* Your cries grew shriller, now well past the point of falling back asleep. *Forty six, forty seven.*

I kicked about with my good foot in the dead leaves and spiders' webs that had accumulated on the doorstep. Located the pink garter balled up in the corner, a little tatty now, a little stained, less elastic and far from pretty. I slipped in the front door and slipped the garter back onto my head like a good girl, trudged up the stairs where I took you in my arms and gave you the comfort you needed. Everything I thought I knew was wrong. As a child, my mother's word had been final, her certainty absolute. Here I was, older now than she was then yet riddled with conflicts, an unstable compound. As new, Sailor, to this world as you were.

THREE

Then I made a friend. You know him. You know his children. Or did once. He was my friend. I needed a friend.

Always be wary when people tell you they *need* something. Let warning bells ring out at that word.

You think you have friends now but you're four years old. They're just other little kids you know. Some of them will in time become your friends, I hope, meaning they will sustain your spirit on a level you don't yet know exists, become part of the complex support structure, the resilient mesh, that in my better moments I hope I am helping to construct around you and, in particular, beneath you, a trampoline floor separating you from the abyss, a diaphragm no less important for survival than your actual diaphragm. And look, I am talking about myself again.

My friend meant to me what your friends will mean to you when you hit your teens. Right now you're entwined in the family unit and that is as it should be, but one day your friends will be more important to you than we are, in your head at least, and you will tell me: Kai said this, or Zane said that – because he'll have some stupid name from the top ten of stupid names, which will indispose me towards the child and his top ten stupid parents before he even darkens my door. Were he called Brian or Dave I would hail him as the son of revolutionaries. You'll experience your first thrill of independence from your friendship with this Nya and you won't need me any more. You will cast off your maternal shackles, venture forth and fuck up, and that's part of the game, the glorious game we are here on this blessed Earth to play, so when I say he was my friend, I mean he was that kind of friend. He was a new era or, in my case, a return to an old one. It's important, when you're a teenager, that you find that freedom, Sailor. And important, when you're a wife and mother, that you don't.

You know what? Let's leave my friend for another day. It was just the relief of sharing the parenting. Well, there was more. He knew me before you, by which I mean he knew the person I have come to think of as more essentially me than the person I am now. Nor did he appear to resent duty's intrusion upon his life. Maybe that's why I was so happy to see him. So that he would let me in on his secret. Although his secret was, I suspect, that he was simply a better person than me.

He was my friend. I needed a friend.

Beware that word.

* * *

All winter I had been sick. A cold, a cough, a virus, another virus. The mother of a toddler cannot take a sick day. I sat on the stairs and blew my nose. The rain had finally stopped. There is no such thing as bad weather, only unsuitable clothing, but you wouldn't wear the unsuitable clothing. I haggled, I cajoled, did the when/then formulation ('*When* you put your wellies on, *then* we can go out and splash in puddles!') until I could do it no longer. I let the wellies drop to the floor, activating the flashing lights in their soles.

'Why did I even buy these? What is the point if you won't wear them?'

'No!' you retorted.

'You even picked them. Because they light up. Don't you want to jump in puddles and light them up?'

'No!'

'You're just gonna shout *no* to everything I say, aren't you?'

'No!'

I picked up my cup. The tea was cold. I put it back on the radiator.

'No!' you yelled, though I hadn't said anything.

'Stop yelling at me,' I said in a perfectly reasonable voice, hoping it was contagious.

'No no *no*!'

'You won't get a smiley face if you don't stop yelling,' I pointed out sadly. 'Six more smiley faces and you get Diesel 10.' It had taken a good fortnight to get the four smiley faces you already had – a year in toddler time. 'Don't you want Diesel 10?'

You paused to consider how badly you wanted Diesel 10.

'Well done! You're back on track for a smiley face! Now, let's get this raincoat on so we can go out and play.'

'No!'

I lowered the raincoat. 'Poor Diesel 10.'

Three more hours until lunch. Maybe I could do your bath in the morning instead of the evening? But then how would I kill the evening?

'*No!*' You ran off.

'What are you even saying no to?' I could hear the sneer in my voice. Your raincoat was draped over my knee. It was a cute little raincoat, rubber-duck yellow, like an illustration in a picture book depicting how childhood should look, except now it was too heavy to lift. The afternoon slump had already set in. I picked up my cup of tea. Still cold.

It had gone quiet. I put down the cup. Silence is the toddler alarm bell. I paced through the house and located you behind the couch. A smell.

'Okay,' I said in a bright voice, steeling myself for battle. 'Let's get a clean nappy on you!'

'No!'

'A nice dry one with no yucky poo in it!'

'No!'

'And then we can splash in the puddles. Then we can have fun! But first we have to get rid of the yucky pooey nappy!' I reached out but you scuttled in further. 'Hey, let's do this thing!' I couldn't keep the exclamation marks coming much longer; not the jolly ones at least. The bad exclamation marks were backing up. They were going to explode. I pulled the couch away from the wall and caught you by the waistband, gathered you up and slung you onto my hip. 'No!' you protested and dug your nails into the back of my hands.

'Stop that! It hurts.' I took hold of your wrists and lugged you, wriggling and screaming, up the stairs.

Your hand shot out again when I laid you on the change table only this time you scraped my cheek. 'What the *fuck*!' I yelled in your face.

The force of my voice shocked us both. I dumped you in your cot and got out of there, kept going until I found myself cornered in the back garden staring at the intersection of the sodden hollow block walls. I had been very close to giving you a slap, Sailor. *That* is how close I had been.

That kid is alright, my friend said the day he met you. I get a good vibe off that kid.

He was my friend.

I needed a friend.

* * *

I unclipped your harness when we made it into the playground after lunch. You sprang out of the buggy, Prometheus Unbound, and belted across the wet rubberised surface. Out came the sun and dried up all the rain. The first twenty minutes in a playground are impeccable, especially when the sun shines. I took a photo, sent it to my husband. Smiley face back.

You tottered about like the town drunk and I tottered after you like the town drunk's mate. Little kids bolted around in all directions, their skulls narrowly missing one another. It was the Hadron Collider in there.

You indicated your desire to be lifted onto the swing. It was the cage-on-two-chains type. I hoisted you in and pulled the seat back like a catapult to propel you into the air. I couldn't see your face, just the back of your head, the breeze in your flossy hair.

Your whoops of excitement abated after a while and we continued in silence, the swing a pendulum marking time. Finally, another child queued behind me, relieving me from duty. I hauled you off and applied you to the bottom of a ladder. Up you chugged. You had to keep moving. It didn't matter what you were moving on. I took a picture of you sliding down the yellow chute and sent it to my husband. Smiley face.

Two plumes of snot shot out of your nose. 'Oops,' I said, getting out a tissue. 'Come here.'

'No!'

I caught you by the hood and clamped the tissue to your face like a chloroform rag. You struggled and broke free. I glanced down at the contents – yellowy green: infection? – then looked up to see you on a collision course with the big kids' swing, which had reached its furthest apex and was now accelerating towards your skull. The woman manning it leapt forward and grabbed it by the chains before it connected with your face, nearly dislodging her own child. We gaped at each other, the woman and I, after you'd sailed obliviously past. I put my hand on my heart and thanked her.

'We've all been there,' I heard her call as I ran after you, and ran after you, and ran after you.

You clambered onto one end of the miniature see-saw. I took the other end. Up and down I lowered and raised you, murder on the thighs. Had I slammed my full weight down, I could have launched you into space.

We found ourselves in front of the spinning carousel, waiting for it to stop. A little girl was already on board. The etiquette surrounding communal rides was awkward at best. The wheel had to be dragged to a halt to allow you to board, then all the *sorry*s and *say thank you*s to the other mother and child. 'I don't want the little boy,' the little girl said to her mother, who told her to be nice.

I stood back and pushed, taking in the little girl. This was an impressive speech for one so small. I enquired after her age. Three months younger than you. 'Wow,' I said, feeling a chill, 'she's very advanced, isn't she?' Her mother smiled ruefully. 'Oh, she never shuts up!' Little girls are so much more articulate than their male counterparts. But don't worry, Sailor: you'll still be paid more than them.

There were almost as many adults in the playground as children. 'I don't remember grown-ups standing around for hours in playgrounds when I was a kid,' I remarked to the little girl's mother, beaming at you whenever your face flashed past. The whole operation was giving me vertigo. 'Only weirdos stared at children back then.' The woman and I had been standing in collegial silence for a while, or long enough for me to conclude that our silence was collegial, the two of us taking turns to push the carousel, our offspring pinned into submission by G-force. I turned to her and found, as I often did, that I was looking into a face a good decade younger than mine. 'The dynamic has changed from us trying to please our parents to us trying to please our children. Have we found ourselves in a period of overcorrection, do you think?'

'Mmm,' the woman murmured.

'Plus there are no adult males in here. Have you noticed that? Not even a grandad (for there were several older women). When it comes to unpaid labour, where are the men? It's gender apartheid in here.'

'Whee!' the woman said.

She extricated herself and her child a minute or two later. The woman had a point: apartheid was overstating it. 'Quicken!' you implored me when they were gone and I spun you faster, harder, until you were a laughing blur. It is impossible to witness joy in your child without your own level rising correspondingly. You need that lift in your day, believe me. Joy is as short as the word. *Check out the bravery of my child!* I wanted to proclaim. *Look at him go!* But there was no one to proclaim it to. I took a photo for your father but you came out smudged.

'Stuck!' you declared and I stopped the carousel. You disembarked and meandered dizzily back toward the swing, which had come free again. A young woman was striding past the brightly painted perimeter fence, an independent female unit. Waisted coat, silk dress, difficult shoes. You could not sprint after a small child in such difficult shoes. It was her turn on the swing now, it occurred to me as I lowered you into the seat. This realisation was stark. It was staggering, in fact. Not the realisation that it was her turn as that my turn was over. Nor was it a matter of joining the back of the queue and waiting for my turn to come around once more. It would never be my turn again.

Oh wow, oh wow, I thought, watching her go. Watching a lot go. Toddlers don't like transitions and neither did I. She had winded me, that girl. That girl who had not registered me, nor the bomb that had detonated in her wake. As I had possibly winded mothers in my day. Simply by walking by. By being free to walk by.

I pushed and I pushed you until it became mechanical, the cogs and gears of a closed system, my hands barely my own. I didn't. Hit you. Earlier when you had scratched my cheek. I had wanted to. I had screamed an obscenity in your face. But I didn't. Hit you. Didn't. Hit you. I pushed the swing to the rhythm of those words. 'Stuck!' you finally yelled.

I checked my watch. We'd clocked in an hour and a half. That should make you sleep. 'Alright, time to go home.' My feet were cold.

'No,' you shouted as I set you down.

I sneezed and you evaded my grasp. 'Come on,' I said, rooting around for a clean tissue, but could only find your dirty one, which I used, 'the birds have gone to bed.'

'No.'

'The bees have gone to bed.'

'No!'

Another sneeze. You and your tusks of infected snot. 'We'll be back tomorrow.' And the day after that, and the day after that again.

'No!'

Oh it was all so stupid. My husband would complain if his dinner was late. He would actually complain. And I would actually want to walk out. The carrots and potatoes were already peeled. I had chopped them and put them into saucepans of water while you napped. '*When* you get in the buggy, *then* you can play with your cars at home.'

'No!'

'Do you give lessons in self-assertion?'

'No!'

'In our day, corporal punishment was legal. Did you know that? If we didn't do what we were told, they hit us.'

'No!'

Did you even know what slapping was? You, who had never seen a cigarette. My childhood was going to seem like the olden days to you. Just as my parents' childhoods were sepia to me. My dad, your grandad, brought us to a white beach one summer's day. He brought us to many beaches when we were kids but this particular trip involved the boat, a small fibreglass river boat that spent most of the year propped upside down against the garage wall growing algae. God knows where it is now. He wheeled it down the slipway and in we jumped wearing orange life jackets on which he'd written our names in black marker. The ink had bled into the coarse fabric.

When we landed on the beach, Dad fired up his camping stove in the lee of a miniature cliff made of sand, a thatch of marram grass sprouting at the top. Sausages were the only thing he could cook. He fried them, then sliced them length-ways onto buttered batch. They melted the butter and were divine. For years I had been telling myself that I must go back to that beach. Now and then it flares up in my memory but I do not know its whereabouts. It exists only so long as I don't go looking for it. If I find it, I will regret finding it because my father as he was then won't be there. It is not the beach that I am hoping to find.

We were the only ones left in the playground. The light was leaching out of the sky. In an hour or so the teenagers would appear, gravitating towards the carousel like zombies. No, they were full of life; I was the zombie dragging my half-dead bones after you. 'Right,' I announced decisively, 'that's it, we're done.'

I wrestled your scrabbling feral cat of a body into the buggy. You pulled Haka faces when I held you down with one hand, fiddling with the harness with the other. But the harness required two hands. As soon as I released your chest, you slithered out. I *can't*, I snapped at my internalised husband. I literally *can't* trap the bloody child in the bloody buggy if the bloody child doesn't want to be trapped because a *man* designed the harness. Only a man could think a parent/guardian has two hands free.

'Get back here!' I was shouting. You're in terrible form, my husband had told me the night before. You're always in terrible form. 'Get back here *now*!'

'No!' You were shouting too. There was nobody around to hear us.

'You'll catch a cold.'

'No!'

'What about my cold? I already have a cold. I'm sick and I want to go home.'

'*No!*'

I sneezed again. No tissue. 'I just want to go home,' I pleaded, feeling very sorry for myself. Imagine heading off like a normal human being, like that girl in the difficult shoes. I laughed out loud, the notion of free will was so absurd. 'It's getting dark!'

'No!'

I dragged you out by your ankles from under the climbing frame, got you by the scruff. You somehow squirmed out of your jacket and shot off, leaving me holding a hood. I chucked the jacket onto the buggy. Fine. I would freeze you out of the playground, if that's what it took.

You darted about in triumph, a woodland sprite in the violet twilight, and I stared at you until it seemed I had imagined you, so implausible you looked, so ill-adapted to our climate, this pale delicate wisp of a pale delicate child who would not survive the night.

I stood waiting for you. As I always stood waiting for you. Your bodyguard, your sentry. My life was passing me by. This was my life. A tree. I stood planted by that playground fence like a tree. Part of the landscape, not notable in itself but for the flower it has borne. All the scenic trees bearing all the scenic children. Those trees seem invulnerable. If one falls, everything falls with it. The whole edifice comes tumbling down. So the tree stands guard, its branches thrown up to the heavens, children perched in them like birds, withstanding whatever the elements throw at it because the tree must.

Finally, you shyly approached, a forest fawn venturing into a clearing, and threw your arms around my legs. 'I sorry, Mama,' you said, a big statement for a small boy, and I reached down to touch your blue cheek. I was sorry too.

'You're frozen.' I picked you up and carried you to the buggy, your arms locked around my neck.

'I luz you,' you said, kissing my face, and then we were doing our thing again, exchanging electrons, the ion stream; whatever it was that felt so good, oh, oh. All I had lost and all I had gained. Poor old Dad, I thought as I strapped you in and turned for home. Poor old Dad with his sausages, his buttered batch bread. His dismay when we hit our teens and wouldn't call him Daddy any more. And would never call him Daddy again. You think this tree that shelters you is unassailable, Sailor, but look again. Even on the stillest of days, every last leaf is trembling.

* * *

Then one day, then one day.

Nothing would do you but to crawl the wrong way up the slide, me lifting you each time another child came flying down the chute, then reattaching you. A man had wandered into the playground. A man in a playground on a weekday is an unusual enough phenomenon and will generally be found poking at his portal to another world, his phone, because he does not want to be there – not because he dislikes being with his children: it's the social awkwardness of a playground that's the killer, as if he has blundered into the ladies' room, which he kind of has. But none of us like playgrounds. Just because they are full of women doesn't mean women like them. Women put up with them, that's the difference.

You screamed. A child had come down the slide while I'd been regarding the man. Two little feet in your face. I snatched you up to let the other little one continue down.

That morning had been so beautiful I was afraid of squandering it. Some day you might know what I mean. April, a tumult of tender new growth after the long hard slog of winter. The imperative to get my fill of summer before it ended although it had not yet begun. To get my fix of whatever it was I thought I needed so badly in my life, that thing, that maddening *thing*, that was missing. When I look back on my own childhood I see summer days, but when I look back on yours I feel cold.

You were bawling again, tears of outrage addressed to the little girl who had collided with you. She stood at the bottom of the slide gaping up at us in alarm. 'It's okay, sweetie,' I assured her over your screams, 'it wasn't your fault.' Her little face crumpled and she let out a wail, at which sound the man, who was stationed in front of the carousel, turned around and approached. Under his arm was a pink toy buggy, comically out of proportion, King Kong clutching the starlet, for he was a tall man, broad shoulders, the kind who finds long-haul air travel an ordeal. He scooped up his sobbing child with his free arm before glancing my way.

'They collided on the slide,' I explained over your racket.

He lowered his sunglasses. 'Soldier?'

Sensing you were losing my attention, you ramped up your screaming. 'Wow! Hey!'

It was my friend.

'Look at you!' Shouting because now his daughter was screaming too. 'A kid and all.'

'Look at us!' Two adults yelling to make themselves heard over two toddlers yelling to make themselves heard. I caught myself fussing at my hair, trying to make it fall nicely which it wasn't going to do because it needed a wash. You were screaming right in my ear. Right in my ear, Sailor, right in my ear. I tried to set you down but you clung to my neck so I took you back up and wished I had make-up on. This was not how he had last encountered me, back then, those days, the ones we failed to get our fill of, or I failed anyway, when it was our turn on the swing.

'Thank Christ,' he said when his child stopped screaming. He put her down and set her up with the pink buggy. You fell quiet to inspect what she was getting that you were not. My friend straightened up. 'Have you just the one?'

'Isn't one enough?'

'One was perfect,' he said with a fondness that bordered on nostalgia.

'Was?'

'Yes, I've three now.'

'Whoa.'

I waited for him to indicate which ones were his, but he didn't, so I had to ask. He squinted and pointed out two more delightful children.

'Three under five? Yikes.'

He shook his head. 'You have no idea. So who's this fine young fella?' he asked, tweaking your dangling heel. 'Look at those big long legs.' I nearly burst with pride. Why does a child's size mean so much to a parent? You beamed at him and he beamed back. 'Well, aren't you the friendly chap.' He used to do that all the time, my friend: compliment you. And a compliment for you was, or felt like, a compliment for me.

My friend turned his attention to me. 'Well?'

'Well.'

He put his hands on his hips. 'You look the same,' he remarked then, and there was not a nicer thing he could have said to me. There was literally not a nicer thing.

'Yeah right,' I countered, 'even recognising me is an achievement.'

'Stop that. You look *exactly* the same.'

'That's a lie, but I'll take it. And so do you.'

'Ach,' he said grimly. 'Ach.'

His little girl was regarding me from the safety of his knee. She had curls the colour of honey, and caramel eyes and was, I thought, just the kind of daughter your father would have melted for. My friend gave her shoulder a squeeze. 'Eye contact, say hello, job done.'

'Hello,' she blinked up at me.

100

'Hello,' I replied but didn't know what to add nor how to pitch it because she was three and I hadn't gotten to that page in childrearing yet. 'We're not supposed to praise little girls for their looks any more,' I told my friend, 'but for their brains, and my God but your daughter is clever. Such clever hair, such clever eyes.' She really was a beauty, that child.

'Gets it from her mother, obviously.'

I jigged you on my hip. 'This is my friend. Say hi.'

You scrutinised him for a moment before making a lunge. My friend instinctively stepped into your hug while I held your legs. 'Aw, thanks, little fella, you've made my day.' You signalled to be put down and tottered over to his daughter.

'Wow, he's friendly.'

'Yup, he's . . . a lot of things.'

Small talk, small talk. Sailor, you are going to lose a lot of your life to small talk, struggling to find something, anything, to say, as you seek a way to broach the real stuff. I hope you are better at it than me.

'Are you well?' he asked.

I had to tilt my head to look up at him. He was even taller than I remembered. Was he thinking the opposite? God, she's shrunk. No. He thought I was *exactly the same*.

'I'm grand, you?' Heels. I used to wear heels. Difficult shoes. *Click clack* about town, not *schlep schlep* around the kitchen. Heels and dresses, finery in general. A different era, a dead civilisation. Deposed monarchs.

'Ach,' he said again, and gestured at the kids. 'Busy.'

I tucked my hair behind my ear and felt ashamed. Of

my sloppy clothes, my coat with the swinging pockets that was essentially a wearable bag, my hollow eye sockets, my unwashed hair. I shrugged up at him. See? You've got me. No fine feathers after all.

'But it's so good to see you,' he said brightly, as if returning to a happier topic. 'It's really good.'

'Yeah,' I nodded back. 'Really good!'

'How long has it been?'

'Aw Jesus, don't ask.'

Screams. We both turned. It was my kid and I went to you, then he went to one of his boys, who was stuck at the top of the rope climbing frame, so my friend had to climb up while I laughed from below, then it was me because you'd mislaid a shoe. And although it was the usual interminable high-drama low-comedy slapstick palaver of keeping pre-schoolers alive, this time it was almost fun.

'Never buy shoes with laces,' he sighed when our Brownian motion paths intersected. He was stooped over his eldest son's foot yet again.

'I don't buy laced shoes for myself any more,' I told him. *Schlep schlep.* 'Who has the time to tie laces?'

'Who has the time,' he concurred, and was gone.

Next thing, he was assembling his children on scooters. I checked my watch. It was going on for five. We'd killed the day. You signalled that you wanted to get up on one of the scooters and his daughter offered you hers. I grabbed the empty buggy and we left the playground as a pack, no mind games, no headwrecks, no tears.

'You don't have to do the hood thing,' I observed when we reached his car. His children stood waiting to be loaded up and belted in.

'What hood thing?'

I indicated your hood, which I held like a dog lead. 'To stop them from bolting.'

'I do not have to do the hood thing.'

'I can't take my hands off him or he'll run away.'

'It's a good sign.'

'That my kid's always trying to get shot of me? How is that good?'

'I don't know! He feels secure without you? Do I look like I know the first thing about parenting?'

'Actually, yes,' I said, indicating his happy, healthy children. Those beautiful children.

Our parting was an extravaganza of awkward gestures and affirmations – *great to see you*, and *so great* and *that's a great little kid you've got there* and *yours are great too*. You threw your arms around his daughter. I took a photo. Didn't send it to my husband. Smiley face. Then you gave my friend's leg a goodbye hug. He picked you up and tossed you in the air. A squeal of delight. 'I get a good vibe off that kid,' he told me. 'That kid is alright.'

He rolled down his window before departing. 'This is a great playground.'

'Just as well,' I said, 'seeing as I practically live in it.'

'Oh yeah? I think we'll come back to this playground.'

'Cool. The kids can have another playdate.'

We waved as the car pulled away, then I transferred you to the buggy. No drama, no fuss, I was back on the swing. *Socialised.*

* * *

'You seem in better form,' my husband remarked that night.

'Do I?'

'You seem happier, more like yourself.'

'I met a friend in the playground.' It sounded like something a four-year-old would say.

'That's great!' he exclaimed, jollying me along as if indeed I were a four-year-old. He treated me like I treated you: ninety seconds away from a nervous breakdown. It had been a while since my husband and I had shared an adult conversation.

* * *

'Ah,' my friend exclaimed happily when I came upon him the following day, parked on the playground bench. He threw out both hands in a *behold* sort of way, clipping the double buggy with his elbow and sending it rolling my way. 'It is you.'

'It is I,' I confirmed, stopping his buggy with my foot.

He stood up and a doll fell from his lap. He bent down to pick it up and bumped his head off the handle of the buggy. 'Thanks,' he said when I laughed.

I picked up the doll and handed it to him. 'No: thank you. You're making me look good here. *Competent.* So thanks.'

My friend's gestures were too big for the things around him, which were too small. It was not a problem he'd had in the old days but here we both were, trapped in a doll's-house world. His clumsiness deflected attention from mine.

I unclipped you from the harness and set you down. My friend's daughter sidled up. The pair of you stared stonily at one another the way little kids do. She really was a clever-looking child, with her tumbling waves of clever hair. It turned out she wasn't his youngest, just his smallest. 'She takes after her mother,' my friend explained. 'My wife is tiny.'

You pottered off with his daughter without a backward glance. I straightened up and watched you go. 'Wow,' I said and sat down beside my friend. 'He's off my hands. What do I do with all this freedom? I still can't go to the toilet unless he's distracted.'

My friend gesticulated at the ground. 'Opportunity knocks. Have a wee.'

He dressed like a grown-up. I liked that about my friend. When we were young, he dressed like a young man, and now that we were grown-ups, he wore grown-up clothes. One of my husband's friends had shown up with a Mr Man T-shirt stretched over his belly and my reaction wasn't hey, here's a fun guy. Mr Immature. That's not what the T-shirt said but that's what I saw. Don't be that guy, Sailor.

'Oops,' said my friend, getting to his feet, 'man down.'

Brownian motion again, him wiping a nose, stopping a fight, putting on a cardigan, me wiping a nose, stopping a fight, taking off a hoodie. Christ on a bike, he would say to his beautiful children, what now? What is it *now*? He didn't put on an act like a woman: the cutie-pie voice, the baby words. He engaged with his children not as a mother might – by encouraging and cajoling and constantly praising – but he engaged just as fully. Ah here, don't give me that, etc, and my suspicion is that he was doing a better job of preparing his children for the adult world than we were – by we, I mean women, and mothers in particular – who were concocting an entirely fake world that would cease to exist the moment we ceased concocting it for them. Because everyone isn't there to help you, Sailor, and nobody actually speaks goochy goo, and you sure as hell won't always be the winner. In fact, the odds are that you will never be the winner because we have raised you as milksops. That was his word, by the way. *Milksop*. His kids laughed whenever he used it, it evidently being some in-family joke. I wanted in on that family. We were better together, my friend and I. Better parents. I was, anyway. I was a better mother to you when I was around my friend. But a worse wife.

'Here,' he said when you fell over and screeched. A plaster. Instead of going, 'Where are the plasters?' as my husband might, knowing his intern had almost certainly neglected to pack them, my friend just passed one across. A small difference and a huge one. I had come to accept, since becoming a mother, that I was incompetent. It had become common knowledge in our home, like starving a fever, but starvation is never the answer. My friend apparently did not see the layers of ineptitude and failure that had accreted upon me, the kitchen slops in my hair. He saw his old pal from the ramp when we used to do a very bad thing called smoking, an activity which seems puzzling now, like driving too fast or going clubbing when you could be tucked up in your bed. Even cake. Gotta lay off them buns in middle age. Eat it, smoke it, stay up all night for it because the memories of the damage you wreak upon your body when you are young will sustain your spirit when you are old.

You reach a point, Sailor, when the fun stops.

It just.

Stops.

You're harnessed to this pram which you push up the hill and back down again all day every day. Sisyphus.

But then.

My friend!

And he was in harness too. And we were pushing those prams up the hill together and it was alright, it was okay.

'Jesus, I have to hand it to you,' I said when I saw that plaster I hadn't even asked for, for your knee that wasn't even cut, it just required a bit of a fuss, 'Paw Patrol plasters? You really do come prepared.'

'Ha!' he said, as if this were a ridiculous prospect. 'You think I am capable of this? I am not capable of this. My wife restocks the bag every night. She'll literally check this box of plasters tonight and make sure there's a selection inside. She cuts up the fruit and stuff in the morning before she goes to work. I just grab the bag and go.'

'Wow. Jealous.' I applied the plaster to your knee. You bent over double to examine it up close before tottering off to find someone to show it to.

'Yeah well, she wants to know they're eating healthily. She knows I'd just give them crisps.'

'Are you still with . . . ?' Her name escaped me. That weapon from college.

'No. God, no. That ended years ago.'

'I'm sorry. Actually, I amn't. She was a—'

'Yup, she certainly was.'

'Your wife sounds great, though. Your tiny wife.'

'She is great. And tiny. She feels guilty about not being with the kids. She's a doctor.'

'Oh wow.'

'Hospital consultant.'

I raised my eyebrows. 'Impressive.'

'I married up.'

'I didn't like to say.'

'Fuck off.'

'You're welcome.'

My friend nudged me. 'Would you look at that.' His daughter was leading you around by the hand. We both got out our phones and took pictures.

'She is insanely cute. Is it wrong to want to steal someone else's kid?'

'Have her. Then it's not theft. Ah Jesus, look at the other one. How many times do I have to tell you,' he called across to his youngest but not smallest, 'if you're going to pick your nose, do it in private.'

The boy took his finger out of his nostril and grinned at me. I grinned back. 'Listen to your father. He's an expert.' The boy sprinted off.

I sat back into the playground bench and listened to the children play, all the scenic children. I listened to their happiness and found I was happy too. 'I'm happy,' I told my friend. Maybe he detected the surprise in my voice. He frowned as if he were hearing something, or trying to. 'Good,' he concluded, 'that's good. That's very, very good,' and although he didn't know the background, I felt he understood it, the significance of this happiness of mine. I might be imbuing him with qualities he didn't possess in my desire for a reservoir in my life, a well to draw on. But I might not.

'I feel like myself again,' I said. 'I feel like my actual self. I've been away a long time but here I am.'

'Welcome back, Soldier.'

'Any smokes in that nappy bag?'

'Are you kidding me? My wife's an otolaryngologist.'

'I'm gonna pretend I know what that is.'

'I've been pretending for years.'

I jumped to my feet. You were climbing the wrong way up the slide again. 'No, we don't do that or we'll hurt ourselves,' I said in the sugar voice, then realised it was a crock of shit. That all your short life, I had spoken to you in a voice that wasn't mine. Such a fuss over paternity tests but who is the real mother, is the question. I'm tired of dissembling, Sailor. This is me. This is what my real voice sounds like. This is who I am.

'I can't bear it that Prince is dead,' he mentioned at some point, pushing the swing or the roundabout or the buggy. I think it was that day. One of the days. 'I just can't bear that he's gone.'

'I can't bear it that Bowie is gone.'

'Oh, wash your mouth out. I can't even think about Bowie yet. Maybe it's death itself I can't deal with. That we will be gone. That this will be gone. That one day they,' he gestured at the children, 'will be gone. I looked at the cherry-blossom petals drifting to the ground this morning, the overabundance of beauty that I find almost painful because I know it can't last, and I thought, *It's great to be not dead!* That's the sentence that popped into my head. Not: *It's great to be alive!* like I did before becoming a father (not that I thought being alive was particularly great when I was young) but *It's great to be not dead!*'

This wasn't exactly how he'd phrased it – drifting blossom, abundance almost painful – but I knew what he meant. That this was our turn on the swing, that our turn would be over.

'I didn't think this way before them,' he concluded, indicating his children. 'But we can't die now, you know? We just can't. Not for another few decades.' He looked at his watch. 'Jesus, I better get the dinner going.'

Yep, I definitely have those words right. *I better get the dinner going.*

'What are you cooking?'

'Just roast chicken.'

Him heading off to cook hot food made me want to traipse

home after him. My friend had it down. He had made a family. It takes a village to raise a child but you only got me. It was French existentialism patrolling those playgrounds before he rocked up. Or do I mean nihilism? Don't go down that road, Sailor. Or go down it when you're fifteen and have a good laugh at yourself afterwards. I'll have a good laugh too.

'Roast chicken,' I said, 'that's an idea. Maybe I'll roast a chicken too.' I looked down at you. 'Do you like roast chicken?'

'Yeah!' Liar.

'Everyone loves roast chicken,' my friend said for your benefit, knowing the difficulties I had feeding you. His smallest but not youngest had those difficulties too.

'Well,' he said before pulling away in the car, 'it's great to be not dead!' He tooted the horn of his big people-carrier full of little people who were all madly waving goodbye. I raised my palm. He raised his in response like we were swearing an oath. Was he thinking what I was thinking? That if we'd both been sentenced to five years without parole, then why not do bird together? 'At ease, Soldier,' he called out the window. I clasped my hands behind my back and loosened my stance. At ease, Soldier, now.

FOUR

The bed was white, wooden and wholesomely old-fashioned. It was a doll's-house bed, only bigger. Which generated reservations. Raising a child was not a game. Games were fun.

I turned to my husband. 'What do you reckon? Is it pandering to late capitalism's commercialisation of motherhood?'

'Hmmm?' he murmured without looking up from his phone.

'Is it promulgating an insidious ideology?'

He frowned. 'Is what?'

'The bed.' What else? We had come to IKEA to buy you a bed. 'What do you think?'

'It's nice.' He shrugged when he sensed more was required. 'It's a bed. What do you want me to say?' His stock response.

'What, like, tell me the words I need to fob you off because I can't be bothered thinking them up myself?'

'Well, what *do* you want me to say?'

'I don't want you to say *what do you want me to say*, like I'm this tyrant who makes people say only what she wants to hear. I'm not Vladimir Putin.'

'I didn't say you were Vladimir Putin. I'm just saying: it's a bed.'

'But maybe we should forget about a toddler bed and go straight to a full single? I mean, he'll get what, two years out of this? Are we just killing the planet?'

'Whatever you think.'

'I'm asking what you think.'

'I trust you. You decide.'

'Don't dress your apathy up as a mark of your trust.'

'What? You're better at this stuff.'

'How am I better? I haven't raised any other kids either. It's his childhood we're building here.'

My husband lowered his phone. 'No: it's a bed.'

You climbed out of the buggy. Relieved of your weight, it tipped over backwards – unbalanced by the nappy bag hanging from its handles – and lay sprawled at our feet like a drunk. I uprighted the buggy, unhooked the nappy bag and swung the strap over my shoulder.

'Isn't this the girls' section?' my husband said, noticing his surroundings now that he'd lowered the phone.

'The duvet is pink but the bed is white.'

My husband nodded at you. 'He's on it.'

'Oh,' I said, and got you down. Only you wouldn't get down. Instead, you shrieked.

'Get him down,' my husband instructed me.

'Do I work for you?' I turned back to you on the bed. 'Get down this minute or The Man will come.' That gave you pause. I had heard another mother in the couch section warning her kids about The Man. So had you. You looked around. No sign of any Man. I pointed at the ceiling. 'He's watching us on the cameras, okay? Get off the bed or he will come. Do you want The Man to come?'

You climbed off the bed. Wow. Something had worked.

'See? You're better at this stuff,' my husband said. 'You look lovely,' he added.

'I washed my hair.' And had put on make-up, amazed by how much healthier I looked.

He grasped the headboard and gave it a rock, kicked the tyres. 'I like the bed,' he pronounced. 'It is a good bed.'

'But should we bite the bullet and go for a regular single bed at this point. Just put, you know, one of those safety-rail things on it.' I looked around for one of those safety-rail things.

My husband rolled his eyes. 'Could you not have decided this before we left the house?'

'We're deciding now. It's a process. Wait, are those ones extendable?'

'Oh good Christ. Get this bed. This bed is fine.'

'*Fine?*'

'Yes, *fine.*'

'You'd just buy the first thing you laid eyes on.'

'Yes, I would. Whatever it takes to get out of here.' Another couple stopped to consider the bed. The woman was heavily pregnant. They had a toddler about your age. The woman said something in a language I didn't recognise and looked at the man. He shrugged.

'You literally couldn't care less, could you?'

'I literally could not. It's Saturday. I don't want to be here.'

'You think I want to be here?'

'You're the one who dragged us here.'

'Because he's growing out of his cot.'

'It's my day off.'

'At least you get a day off.'

To which he retorted with another of his incredibly aggravating stock responses. I can't think of it right now. Not *Relax*. The other one.

I looked down at the flossy crown of your head. Your parents were bickering again. A big boys' bed! I had told you that morning to secure your co-operation. We're gonna buy you a big boys' bed! This was a red-letter day. 'Do you like the bed?'

The flossy head nodded.

'Are you ready for a big boys' bed?'

You tilted your face up to mine. 'Yeah!'

'Will we get this bed?'

'Yeah!'

'Let's do it,' my husband said. 'Let's get this big boy the big boys' bed!'

You jumped up and down with glee. Ah, the warm surge of maternal hormones. I bent down to kiss your head. 'Good boy.' I wrote down the code of the bed and we pushed on.

Except you didn't. I turned around. You were standing by the bed, your little face fallen. The pregnant couple had been replaced by another couple, also with a large bump on board. They had three other kids swarming around them, maybe four.

'Come on,' I instructed you.

You shook your head. 'My bed.'

I smiled. 'Oh no, sweetie, this is the shop's bed. Your bed is a brand new one the same as this but in a box. We have to go downstairs to collect your bed.'

One of the swarming kids climbed on the bed. *My* bed,' you told him.

'Help me out here,' I said to my husband. When this was met with silence I turned around. He was gone. 'Come on,' I wheedled, '*your* bed is waiting for you in the warehouse. Let's go get it!' I bent down to pick you up.

You took a hold of the headboard. 'No!'

'Oh Jesus.' I hadn't the energy.

'What's the delay?' My husband was back. 'Why are we still here?'

'My bed!'

'He thinks this is his bed.'

'This is the show bed,' he told you, like that meant anything to a toddler. 'Your bed is in the warehouse. Come on. Let's go.'

'MY BED,' you yelled. 'MY.'

'Stop that,' he warned you, 'or The Man will come and take you away.'

A look of horror crossed your face.

'Daddy's just being silly.' I gave my husband a vicious glare. 'Daddy's just being a dick,' I muttered to him. 'Again.'

My husband appealed to the ceiling. 'Oh Jesus Christ, can we not just fucking move through the fucking store like a normal fucking family?'

'You haven't eaten, have you?'

'I didn't think it was going to take all day.'

'Who goes to IKEA on an empty stomach?' I dug a tub out of the nappy bag. 'Here.'

'What's that?'

'Apple segments.'

'I don't want apple segments. I want a packet of ham.' He handed the tub back.

'Please don't reject healthy food in front of our child. How about a rice cracker? Or some raisins?' I produced different tubs.

My husband shook his head and walked away. I looked down at you. 'Do you want a rice cracker? Or some raisins.'

You shook your head and followed him.

Result. We had successfully exited the bed section. I put the tubs away.

'There's a very good little boy,' I remarked as I joined the flow of bodies progressing sluggishly along the central aisle. 'Look at this good little boy,' I said to my husband. 'Have you ever seen a little boy as good as this?'

My husband was holding your hand. 'He's a very good little boy, alright,' he confirmed. 'I'd say he must be one of the best little boys in Ireland.'

The self-conscious swagger in your walk indicated that you were taken with this version of yourself. 'I big boy,' you corrected us and we smirked over your head.

'You do,' my husband said to me, and I frowned. 'Look lovely.' He leaned over you to kiss my cheek. For a whole moment we looked like a cohesive family unit.

'Don't touch that,' I blurted when you let go of his hand to reach for a toilet seat. 'Yucky.'

'It's not a real toilet,' my husband said.

'It's the principle.'

'Come on,' he said, trying to hustle you along. 'It's too hot in here.'

'Take off your coat.'

We were all wearing coats. We were all too hot. I unzipped yours and chucked it into the buggy, unbuttoned mine. My skin was prickly. I sneezed into the crook of my arm.

'I feel like shit,' my husband said, as if he were the one who had sneezed.

Then you sneezed. I put my hand on your forehead. 'He has a slight temperature.'

My husband put his hand on his forehead. 'So do I. See?' He scraped back his hair to show me his temperature.

'I'm your wife, not your mother,' I pointed out. If you ever hear these words, Sailor, take a step back. I don't know why men find the distinction so confusing. 'I feel like shit too, alright?' There was no question of anyone putting their hand on my forehead. I had discovered that the hard way after giving birth. I got a tissue out of the nappy bag to clean your nose.

'I get just two days off, you know?' my husband was complaining. 'I get just two days off a week and I have to waste one of them in IKEA?'

'Two whole days? I haven't had a day off since he was born. Unless we count the time I was hospitalised with pneumonia.

119

And then you got your mother in.'

He sneezed so loudly then – a declarative *I am sneezing* sneeze – that the two of us jumped, then he rolled his eyes mournfully to me, as if I was thinking: oh my poor husband, when actually I was thinking: it's a sneeze, try giving birth. Read the room, Sailor. Learn to read the room.

Then I sneezed again. You had woken three times that night, maybe four. Stumbling through the darkness to pick you up, *Wheels on the Bus* until the crying stopped. 'Don't keep going into him,' my husband retorted when I pointed out how tired I was. 'You give him too much attention.'

'You cannot give an infant too much attention. It's not possible. I've read studies about this.' I hadn't. Or maybe I had – the phrase seemed dimly familiar. Either way, I was on safe ground quoting infant studies to your father. If there was one thing he couldn't refute, it was an infant study, having never read one.

Down in the basement I grabbed a shopping trolley. 'I'll stop you there,' my husband said. 'In and out, no dicking around.' I turned and put it back.

'I had to be carried home in a chair once,' I told him. 'I mean, I don't remember it because I was too young but we had this little wicker chair in the house and my parents told me I took a shine to it in a shop on holidays and I wouldn't get out of it so they bought it. They carried me back to the car in it.'

My husband shot me a smile. 'Little madam.'

I pointed at a picture frame that had spaces for four photographs. 'How do people find time to print up photographs? Seriously.'

He pointed at a doormat that said HOME. 'For those who can't tell their house from the bank?' Then he checked his phone. 'There's no signal down here.'

'They have Wi-Fi.'

'What's the code?'

'Yeah, because I know it by heart.'

'Ask one of the salespeople.'

We looked around. No salespeople. 'Alternatively, you can leave the damn thing alone for ten seconds?'

He sighed. 'I'm *working*.'

His Get Out of Jail card. I sighed back.

A stand of lamps shaped like toadstools. I picked one up. 'This would look good in his room.' No trolley to put it in.

'My,' you called up, reaching for the lamp.

'It's not a toy.'

'My!'

A heavily pregnant woman picked up the same lamp. The one with all the kids.

'*My!*' you shrieked.

'Oh sweet Jesus,' said my husband. 'Let's just get out of here.'

'Should you get your blood sugars tested?' I asked him over your yells. 'Is that what's going on here? Do I need to google blood sugars?'

'You can't,' he informed me. 'There's no signal.'

'My, my, *my*!'

I bent down to let you touch the toadstool. 'See? It doesn't do anything. It's not a toy.'

My husband picked up a lightbulb.

'Don't get that. It's not bayonet.'

He pointed at the toadstool. 'It's for that. Screw top.'

A kid glided past in a shopping trolley. Nine or ten but already he had a fat head. And a phone. I looked at the parents. 'How can a child have a fat head?' I remarked when they were out of earshot.

My husband bopped me with the lightbulb. 'Cancelled.'

We rejoined the funeral cortège and proceeded through the store at a stately pace. 'If our kid's head got fat,' I muttered, 'I would regard myself as a failed parent. Because it's not the kid's fault. The parents control the kid's diet and life-style at that age.'

The kid was dressed in a football kit. This raised a number of questions.

'Why is it,' I asked my husband, because he knew sport, 'that unfit people wear more athletic gear than fit people?

'And doesn't that poxy English football team stuff cost a fortune? Like, why does it cost so much to look so poor?

'Why is he even wearing an English kit? We're not in England.

'What's so wrong with an Ireland jersey?

'Why don't they take the kid out of the trolley and make him walk?

'How'd they even get him in the trolley?

'Ha, how are they gonna get him back out?' A crate of long white plastic objects caught my eye. Were they cling-film dispensers? Was a whole major ball-ache in my life about to be resolved?

'Look,' said my husband, 'our child is just so skinny that he makes other kids look fat.'

'So you're saying it's our child that's wrong?'

'You know that's not what I'm saying. Stop twisting my words.'

'You're criticising his weight, and therefore criticising my inability to get him to eat. Because yeah, I'm sure our child would eat nuggets and sausages if let.'

'Well, maybe you need to lighten up on the healthy eating once in a while. Bad food being better than no food at all?'

I stopped. 'Do you want to take over? Seeing as I'm making such a total bags of it.' Your father wouldn't know what you ate nor when you ate it. Like many men, he thought changing nappies qualified him as an involved father.

He took my hand. 'You may be a fat-shamer, and I don't know what possessed you to think our marriage would survive flat-pack furniture, but our son is a very lucky boy to have a mother like you.'

I looked askance at him, gauging sarcasm levels, but he was gazing at me the old way, the soft way, the way which made everything okay. He squeezed my hand and I squeezed his hand back. A pang then to see my wicker chair again. That artefact from my childhood, an earthenware shard, to glue it back into place and shore myself up. I put my arm around his waist and he pulled me in close. In the old days, I'd have made him a honey and lemon drink if I heard him sneeze. I wouldn't have fought it, would simply have offered it to him, and he would have put his hands around the heat of the cup and smiled. Then we would both have felt good, felt loved, and returned to the conversation about having a child.

My husband looked down. Then he looked into the buggy. 'Where is our child?'

'Is he not in the buggy?' I looked into the buggy.

'No, I told you to watch him so I could get the lightbulb.'

'No, you didn't.'

'Yes, I did!'

'No, you absolutely didn't.'

'Yes, I absolutely did.'

'If I did not acknowledge the instruction, I didn't hear it. Okay? If I did not respond in any shape or form, it's because I did not hear the instruction.'

'Seriously,' he said, 'where is he?' He turned and went one way. I went the other.

I battled my way upstream against the current of human bodies to the last place you'd been seen, the toadstool stand.

There was no little boy at the toadstool stand. I ditched the lamp and threaded my way through the many display stands. You were so small, you could have been hidden behind any one of them.

I called your name, not that you ever came to me. I called it over and over, hysteria rising in my voice. Other people looked around too, trying to be helpful, though they did not know who they were looking for. I pushed through a door marked *Shortcut* and found myself in a hall of mirrors. Fake windows on the wall, fake sunlight streaming through venetian blinds, toilets that weren't plumbed in. You were just getting your head around the world and I bring you here? To this confounding place?

I doubled back through the shortcut door. Instead of collecting my scattered earthenware shards, I was breaking up into smaller ones. I combed through a random cluster of kids. Then I was back at the stairs leading up to the showrooms. I raced up them and through the rooms in search of the bed you thought was your bed, knowing as I did so that a toddler could not have climbed those stairs unassisted. Apart from anything, someone would have stopped you. Another mother would have stopped you.

Back down to the basement. 'I've lost my child,' I told a member of staff, a girl so young she couldn't possibly understand. 'He's nearly two. But he's small for his age. He doesn't eat.' Why was I telling her this?

As I ran through aisles, scenarios ran through my head. There is a scenario that is worse than the dead-child scenario and that is the missing-child scenario. Because you do not know what is happening to the missing child. All you know is that your child is suffering the worst fate you can imagine. The fate I won't go into. The black net, or deep net, whatever it's called. Darknet.

And you? Mister Adventurer. You'd go off with anyone.

If I was going to abduct a child, if I was going to despoil

one, I'd abduct the one with the most to despoil. I'd abduct the liveliest, the most tempestuous, the hardest to break. I'd abduct you.

I pushed through another shortcut. Storage solutions, shelves. Yelled your name, added a *please*. I turned back but the shortcut was not where I had thought to find it, as if the wall had sealed up.

Back into the mire of human traffic, the maddeningly slow herd, picking things up and putting them down, picking them up and putting them down. What were we all doing in here?

Trying to live. That's all we were doing. Trying to make homes so we could live. Must we be punished?

Into this stream of humanity I had released your hand. The current had carried you away.

Dungeons, cellars. Begging for your mother. Your mother begging for you.

Your screams, when I finally heard them, were as significant as your birth cries, confirming you were alive.

'Oh you fucking cunt,' I uttered, appalled – almost awed – to hear that word pass my lips. Insanity. Relief. Relief. Insanity.

We converged on the huddle of people simultaneously, your father and I. 'Over there,' he called, and I elbowed my way through into an arena of sorts, a space charged by expectancy, people waiting for something to happen – or for something else to happen – because something already had happened: a small child had been lost and a culprit must be found. I ran and snatched you up, the child the child the child, the glorious beloved child. You twisted around to look past me and screamed louder.

'Are you his mother?' the security guard asked me over your howls.

'Yes!' I shouted back. Someone had given you a teddy, a stuffed Dalmatian, which you clinched in a headlock. 'It's okay,' I reassured you, 'it's okay, I'm here,' but you weren't responding. It was like you were blind. For a horrible second I thought you were. I turned to my husband and found not his face but the faces of strangers. I tried to shield you from their stares.

'My mama!' you screamed.

'I'm here. I'm right here.' I smoothed your hair out of your eyes but you still couldn't see me. Again, I glanced around for my husband. Again, the faces. What is it about humans when we stand in a circle? Why are we so bloody ominous, with our gladiators and our blood sacrifices and our death by social media. It was my child they were bearing down on. 'My mama!' you kept screaming like I wasn't there, or worse: like I wasn't your mama.

The crowd was not dispersing. It's not every day you get to watch a small child practically convulsing in fright, and a final act that is far from conclusive. I needed to get you away from those harsh lights and fake rooms. No matter which way I turned, you re-orientated your body like a compass needle to a point beyond me. It was the security guard. You were screaming *My mama* at the security guard, who was not backing off. And why would he? This was hardly the joyful reunification scene of mother and child that the crowd demanded.

The Man, I suddenly realised. The security guard was The Man. The Man who was going to come and take you away, or whatever dumb flippant thing your dumb flippant father had threatened.

'This isn't The Man, pet,' and only when I had said it three or four times did you flick your wild eyes to mine. 'Oh poor darling, there is no Man, that was just pretend, I have you now.' You crumpled into my neck and bawled, the pitch decompressing from terror to reproach. A sense in the background of the crowd standing down. I collapsed on a display chair and rocked you back and forth.

My husband thundered up and thrust a finger in your face. 'Never run off on us again, do you hear me?'

'Leave him.'

'Jesus Christ, that's after nearly killing me.' He held out his hand. It was shaking.

And here was the fat kid in his trolley again, now at my level, blank-eyed, chewing. I glanced up at the father who had slowed down to gawp at us. Blank-eyed, chewing.

I watched them go. 'Is it me?' I asked tightly. 'Am I a body fascist?'

'At least Mr Fat knew where his kid was the whole time,' your father quietly pointed out.

'Yeah, you couldn't miss him.'

I got to my feet. When we finally found the buggy, you wouldn't release my neck, so I carried you through the rest of the shop, past the outdoor candles and picnicware, fire pits, hammocks, items infinitely more aspirational than diamonds or luxury cars because when would there be time for leisure? Getting through the day was as good as it got, as good as it was going to get.

We emerged through double doors into an aircraft hangar of metal shelving units. The two pregnant women were already there along with several other familiar faces, as if we'd all disembarked from the same flight. Everyone hungry now, everyone tired and cross. A wandering tribe who had set out together at the shiny end of the store, an image in our heads of a bright new feather for our nest – in our case, a small white bed in which our baby would sleep and dream and grow happy and strong. Now here we were on the other side, exhausted passengers disgorged into baggage reclaim to scrabble around for our stuff. All we wanted was to go home. But first we had to make the home. The ordeal of flat-pack furniture assembly hadn't even started yet.

'Bless you,' said my husband when I sneezed. But then I sneezed again, and again, until there was no point in blessing me, I was sneezing so much. I was sick and tired of being sick and tired. 'I thought buying our child his first bed would be a nice family thing for us to do,' I said, then laughed at my naivety. That kind of bitter laugh. You know the one. I don't like it any more than you do. It had been lovely, so very lovely, preparing your nursery before you were born, assembling the components like it was a treasure hunt – get this baby monitor, get that cot mobile – my husband and I standing hand in hand over your crib, imagining you in it, beaming at the empty space. I wish you could have seen that. Instead you arrived into the war room, everyone shouting at everyone else. Everyone in your world was me back then. Everyone else was your father.

'Look, forget the bed,' I decided. 'Let's just get out of here.'

'My bed!' you shrieked. '*My bed!*'

'What's the code?' my husband asked and I stared at him uncomprehendingly. 'The shelf number. For the bed.' There was no energy in his voice. No reproach either. Just resignation. In his hand was the lightbulb but I no longer held the lamp.

I reached into my back pocket for the slip of paper. It was empty. I put you on the other hip to check the other back pocket. Then both front pockets. 'I've lost it,' I admitted. 'It's gone.'

'Why didn't you take a photo of it?'

I tilted my head at him, jutted my chin. 'Why didn't you? Why is it always on me? Why didn't you come forward to claim your child back there? Why do I have to be the bad mother who lost her kid? He has a bad father too.' My husband had hung back with the crowd of condemners, swelling their number.

I jigged you up and down, urging you to stop howling about your stupid bed, as I waited for my husband to retaliate. *Here we go*. That was his other stock response to my complaints, the touchpaper to my fuse. I was primed and ready to explode. *Here we go:* BAM!

Instead, he turned and walked away. Because he could.

Your screams engulfed me until I was reeling. I tremble to your frequency, Sailor, a tuning fork, whether I want to or not. Flocking birds change direction simultaneously in flight. To the casual observer, such consonance is beautiful. But the consonance is not beautiful and the sea is not glittering and this bear isn't dancing. Look at us, herding our babies around, our squalling and hungry and fretting babies, our goats and our tents and our chattels. Pitifully, relentlessly, inescapably human. We'd been at this forever and we'd be at this forever. Did it have to be so hard?

FIVE

'I know it's just a bed,' I said. 'But it's his first bed. I wanted to get it right. You know? Like, what size beds do your kids sleep in?'

'Oh don't,' my friend practically yelped. 'Don't open that can of worms.' He scratched his head and crossed his legs and brushed something invisible off his knee before folding his arms and finally hugged himself. 'They won't sleep in their own beds so the two boys sleep with me in the erstwhile marital bed and your woman sleeps in my wife's bed, or, rather, my wife sleeps in her bed.'

'Oh,' I said.

'Exactly: *Oh*. The pair of them in a frilly pink princess bed. Which is a standard single, no safety rail, since you ask.'

'No wonder you're tired.'

'At least your child is sleeping in his own bed. *Bualadh bos* for you.'

A tinkling sound reached our ears and my friend rolled his eyes. 'I swear to God, these pricks are following me around.' His kids came racing up from different corners of the playground. 'Not those ones.' An ice-cream van appeared around the corner. 'This shower.'

'Ice cream, ice cream!' his kids shrieked.

'Ice cream, ice cream,' you chimed.

My friend stood up and dug a fistful of change out of his pocket.

'You know until now,' I pointed out, 'this fella thought the ice-cream van was the Music Van. Didn't you, darling? Isn't that what you thought? Come to play music for the kids?'

'Ice cream,' you asserted.

'Death of innocence,' pronounced my friend as he counted out coins on his palm. 'Ask your client if he wishes to come for ice cream?'

'Do you wish to come for ice cream?'

'Ice cream,' you asserted again. Funny how you could talk when it suited you.

I followed my friend through the playground gate. The ice-cream van was parked across the road. You made a run for it and were garrotted by your collar since I held your hood. My friend's kids, meanwhile, without being told to, had taken one another's hands to form a chain. Seeing this, you took his oldest son's hand on one side and mine on the other, and the six of us crossed the road together, one big happy family.

* * *

Back at the playground, my friend scattered a selection of toys at our feet to buy us time. The four of you descended on them like pigeons. 'I'd kill for a smoke,' he sighed as he lowered himself onto the bench.

You were moving in on the digger that his youngest boy was playing with. There would be unpleasantness. His child was going to cry. And then his child did cry. I stood up.

'Let them work it out,' my friend said.

I tried to prise the digger out of your grasp. 'Sit down,' said my friend. 'Sit down. Just sit down. You're still not sitting down.'

I sat down.

'They'll figure it out themselves. We're trying to raise adults here.' The boy came up to complain about the theft. 'Deal with it yourself,' my friend told him. 'I'm not your solicitor.'

A scuffle ensued. The digger went skidding across the playground and crashed into the fence. 'Fucking hell,' said the eldest boy.

The fight stopped. All the kids turned to gape at the boy. His father sat up. 'What did you say?'

The boy looked alarmed. 'I didn't say fucking hell.'

'You better not have. Now go on. Play.'

'You know what?' I said when play had resumed. 'I'm not as bad a parent as I thought.'

'I'm glad I make you look good by default.' He rubbed his eyes. 'Why does exhaustion manifest in the eyeballs?' He knuckled them until I couldn't watch any more.

Screams. His youngest boy was on his face again. 'Why does that fucking child keep falling over?' he wondered as we made our way across. 'This is, like, the third time today I've had to pick him up.' He set the little guy back on his feet and told him he was grand.

I pointed. 'His shoes are on the wrong way around.' You came over to examine the shoes.

'Ah,' said my friend. 'Silly Daddy.' He carried his boy back to the bench and switched the shoes around. 'Actually, I don't think they are his shoes. Do they seem a little big to you?'

I squeezed the toe: empty inch. Clown shoes. 'Better too big than too small?' I offered. The kid shot off and tripped once more. We shouldn't have laughed.

My friend knuckled his eyeballs again as we trudged back over. 'Is it like eyeball dehydration? What's that goo in your eyeballs called? Glaucous something? Aqueous?'

'I was out sick the day we did eyeballs.'

He uprighted his son. 'Maybe the goo needs sleep to regenerate? I'm so tired I'm almost stoned.'

'Milksop. I suppose we could google it but then we'd be the bad parents for looking at our phones. But then again, we already are the bad parents.'

'No, we're not,' he said vehemently. He lowered his knuckles to look at me with those tired red eyes. 'We're the ones who are *here*.'

'Okay,' I said.

He retreated to the bench to rub his eyes some more. 'Once I had a hangover this bad.'

'I find that hard to believe.'

He kept on rubbing, hunched right over, elbows on knees, and for a moment I thought he was crying. I put my hand on his shoulder. 'You okay?'

He looked up at me and smiled with a raw red face. 'You're a great friend. You know that? You're a great friend to me. Thanks.'

Huh. It never occurred to me that a father would need a friend. Fathers had all the cards. Everything was stacked in their favour. So I'd thought.

'Fuck's sake,' he said when his boy fell over yet again. A passing woman glared at him and chivvied her charges away. 'I can't *talk*,' he said, eyeing her. 'I can't even *talk* any more. It's like having your phone tapped. Plus my back aches, bending over these miniature dictators all day.'

'Try giving birth.'

'You win.'

'Do I, though? Can I ask you a question?'

'Go on.'

'Do you want to be here? Minding your kids full time?'

'Hmmm,' he said. 'Well, they are the most important thing in my life, obviously.'

'Obviously. They are paramount.'

'The kids are paramount. This specific bit is okay: being out with my kids in the park is great.'

'The park is great,' I agreed.

'The park is great. It's the rest of it that kills me, like which fucking shoe belongs on whose fucking foot. It's all so fucking manual and I can't get any work done. I thought I'd get work done while they went out and played, only kids don't go out and play any more, not without a security detail. So I suppose I'm here because my wife wants to be here herself and I'm the next best thing. They howl for her attention when she comes home. They peck at her like little birds. Does that happen to your husband?'

'He's fast asleep by the time my husband comes home. I don't think he really registers his absence. I mean, he's not absent, as such. He just works long hours. You guys see more of each other than they do.'

'That's tough,' said my friend.

You barrelled up to brandish the digger in my friend's face. 'Wow!' he said, 'you got the digger! Good work.' He picked you up and tossed you in the air and you squealed. 'In the time of chimpanzees, I was a monkey. Isn't that right, buddy?'

'Silly Daddy,' you told him and no one quite knew what to say.

* * *

'He says I undermine him,' I found myself complaining as we walked the kids. His two boys rode on ahead like medieval heralds on their glinting scooters. His daughter pushed you in her toy buggy, or tried to. We kept having to stop to tuck your leg back in. 'With the childcare. But, like, any time I give my husband a set task – bedtime, nappy change or whatever – he deliberately fucks up. So there's roaring and shouting but when I intervene, I'm "undermining" him. I may as well do it myself in the first place. So then I'm not only angry with my husband: I'm angry with myself for being his enabler. His golf buddy even said it to me when the pair of them got back one Sunday after a boys' weekend: "We do this because you let us." He was smirking. Like: *they know!* They know they're doing it! But somehow I'm the dick for enabling their dickology. Somehow, it's on me. Maternal gatekeeping or whatever. How am I supposed to end sixty thousand years of male oppression?' I had plucked that number out of the air.

My friend maintained a dignified silence, an art I never mastered. Too late I realised I had slipped into the role I filled at home: the whiner. Some are born whiners, Sailor, but some have whining thrust upon them. We stopped to tuck your leg back into the toy buggy.

'Golf,' he eventually said.

'Golf,' I confirmed.

'*Golf*,' my friend said again.

'Golf,' I confirmed, the word satirising itself. 'It's a work thing. "Networking."' I made air quotes.

'Wow, you married a proper grown-up too.'

'Why, does your wife play golf?'

'God, no. She hasn't the time. She's on call most weekends.'

'At least that's work. Though apparently golf is too. Apparently it's the way to "get ahead".' Air quotes again.

'It's the first thing I look for in a professional. A good handicap.'

'How can a handicap be good?'

He flashed me a smile. 'This is why we're friends.'

We stopped and we stopped and we stopped to tuck your leg back into the toy buggy.

'So now,' I continued, 'when a father of young kids is really good at golf or cycling or some other time-consuming hobby, I'm like, well done you for abandoning your family.'

'I feel we're beginning to get somewhere here,' he concluded. And although I wasn't sure where that somewhere was, I felt we were getting there too.

His boys circled back, complaining of hunger. We set up shop on the next bench. My friend opened a tub of mandarin segments and one of raspberries. His two boys dove in. He proffered the tubs to you and you took fruit from both but stood there holding a piece in each hand. I could feel myself willing you on to eat. His little girl popped a segment of mandarin into her mouth. 'Yum,' she said. 'Yum,' you repeated and ate one too. Same with the raspberry. I beamed at my friend although he couldn't have known what an ordeal lunch had been that day. Three teaspoons of food. Another three at breakfast. I didn't know what to do any more. You looked so wan beside his children. I could see your skull through your haze of hair.

My friend produced three bottles from the backpack and handed them out. I dug out yours. His daughter cried because she wanted the Mickey Mouse bottle and he'd given her the Toy Story one. 'It's the same drink,' he said. 'Everyone has the same drink. Everyone has water.' But still she cried so he took the Mickey Mouse bottle from her brother and gave it to her, giving her brother the Toy Story bottle, whereupon he cried. 'Christ,' he sighed. 'This generation is our revenge on snowflakes.' He performed another switch with a conjuror's flourish, this time involving the third kid and his Lego Batman bottle, then another switch again, co-opting your Tigger bottle into the game. 'Ta-da!' he said when the switches were complete. There was peace for a moment as the dust settled, or maybe it was confusion. He raised an eyebrow at me.

I was in a state of glee: you were drinking water because his kids were. You were eating fruit because his kids were. You were manageable because his kids were. Then his daughter threw her bottle onto the ground because it still wasn't Mickey Mouse.

'This is what'll be paying our pensions,' he said, gesturing at the four pissed-off faces. You were pissed off because his kids were.

'We'll end up in the workhouse,' I said.

'Bet they won't even visit us.'

I liked it. The whole us against them thing.

'I'll visit you, Daddy,' his oldest boy said.

'I'll visit you, Daddy,' his daughter said.

'I visit you, Daddy,' his youngest son said.

'I visit you, Daddy,' you said.

His youngest boy whipped around. 'This no your daddy,' he told you indignantly. 'This my daddy.' He gave you a shove, knocking you onto your bottom. Howls.

I picked you up. 'Your daddy's in the office,' I explained, like that meant anything to you. Like it meant anything to me. I'd never been.

My friend was bollocking his youngest when you broke from me to take a run at him. The boy landed on one of the scooters and, when my friend uprighted him, blood was dripping from his nose. At the sight of it, his daughter freaked.

My friend picked up his injured boy and carried him away. His daughter ran wailing after them. The oldest boy glanced at us before following. And then it was just you and me again. 'I sorry, I sorry, I sorry!' you chanted, tears sprouting from your eyes. As I administered a good sound dressing down, it was sympathy as much as anything that rose in my chest. Oh Sailor, I thought, the little size of you. This is what it feels like when everything goes wrong, and by your own hand. When you are caught, cornered, the one to blame, when you discover something in your nature that you did not know was there and which you do not like. You know what, though? Confusion, shame, resentment, regret: it's my area. Don't panic. Sit tight. I can help you with this.

* * *

You were sitting on my friend's knee. It was a hot afternoon. Same bench, different day. It had been a hectic couple of hours in the playground but now there was a lull. This is what I chiefly recall of the day: the lull. Birdsong, dappled light, a man, woman and child sitting together in the lull which had descended upon them. No one was talking. The people around me gave up on talking once you were born. They stopped exchanging ideas and thoughts; they just made noise. Constant, unrelenting, peevish noise. Not us. We three didn't make a sound.

The breeze moving through leaves is one of my favourite sounds. The breeze was gently weaving through the branches overhead but everything at ground level was drowsy and still. The sun beat down on my outstretched legs. You were perched on my friend's knee, driving your car along him. This had been going on for some time.

My friend and I would look at one another and then we would look at you. Then back to one another. I wanted so much to be left just sitting there with him that I almost said it. 'I just want to sit here in the sun with you. That is all I want.'

His children were in the playground. All the scenic children. Those happy beautiful children. It would start up again. The whole racket would crank back up. But until then, we had this lull.

You were more interested in my friend that day than in the playground or his kids. That was a first. Of the many things you wanted to explore, you most wanted to explore him. His broad shoulders, the contours of his jaw. My friend was terra incognita. Terra incognita means a place that has not yet been mapped, Sailor. An unknown or unexplored region. You drove your car up his chest then circumnavigated his neck. This manoeuvre involved wrapping your arms around him.

A dandelion seed head bobbed along, the kind we used to believe were fairies.

His children darted after a butterfly.

A delighted dog, head stuck out the window of a passing car, tongue tossed back like a scarf.

My friend was wearing a blue gingham shirt, sleeves rolled up. I could smell the fabric conditioner. Around and around his neck your little car went. It was mesmeric, watching you touch him, your hands uncharacteristically gentle. 'Gentle,' I used to instruct you when you petted dogs too enthusiastically. 'Gentle, gentle!' It was several years later before I realised you thought *gentle* meant *stroke*. 'Can I gentle the dog, Mama?' Yes, but always ask the owner first.

You wrapped your arms around my friend's neck and then kissed his face in that way toddlers do, not a peck so much as a suction cup. 'Sorry,' I said and went to pull you off.

'It's okay. Don't apologise for your child. He's an explorer. I miss them.'

'What?'

'Babies. Infants.'

'Really?'

'I do. I'd have more if I could.'

'Huh.' I would have loved a little sister for you. Bet you didn't know that, Sailor. She had a name and all. I almost cried thinking of her last night.

But I didn't cry. I fell asleep.

And nobody woke me bawling during the night. So I was better able to love the child I did have when I woke up feeling human this morning.

You pulled at the neck of my friend's shirt to peer down. I caught a glimpse of his chest. One of the many irritating things about fathers is that their bodies stay the same. Childbirth wreaks no havoc upon them.

You dropped the car down his shirt. He yelped at its coldness then you plunged your hand down after it. I tried to detach you but you shrieked and my friend said, leave him, he's fine. He intercepted the car at the waistband of his jeans, pulled out his shirt to free it, returned it to you. I sat back in the sun.

'How are you?' my friend asked then, and not in a casual

way, not as a variation on hello but as a considered enquiry into my well-being inviting a considered response. His manner of emphasising certain words: How *are* you? It was such a lovely way he had, that ability of his to compress fondness into his voice. Some people have these qualities. Be one of them, Sailor. Have I told you this before? It bears repeating.

'How *are* you?' I could feel his eyes on me.

I am tired. I am lonely. I have found myself mired in resentment in this new life, become a person I don't wish to be, feeling constant guilt for not feeling constant gratitude for the blessing that is my child. I do feel constant gratitude: I adore my child. But I am tired. I am lonely. I am lost.

'Ah, you know,' I shrugged. 'How about you?'

He shrugged back. 'Same.'

I wondered whether he could detect fondness in my voice and, indeed, whether you could, because surely it was better for you to be around warmth and goodwill than your parents' relentless bickering. These were the things I wondered about on that bench. When you were born, you didn't enter my world: I entered yours. I crawled through the small door that had appeared in the wall and there you were, oh my God, perfect. It took me some time to realise your father was no longer with us, not quite. He was there in the beginning but at some point wandered off, stepping out to make a phone call from which he never fully hung up, popping his head in from time to time to see how we were doing, would we like a cup of tea? It was just you and me on our own in there for a while, and then it was you and me and other infants

145

and their carers. Then one day I noticed a man surrounded by things that were too small for him, things he tripped over or snapped in two with his clumsy male strength, a man soothing tears, a man kissing boo-boos better, a man being – I almost said – a woman.

'Do you remember the old days?' I asked him.

An instant smile. 'I remember the old days.'

'They were exciting. Do you remember the exciting people?'

'I do! I remember the exciting people. The people doing exciting things.'

'Wearing ironical clothes.'

'Yes! Those clothes they wore were ironical.'

'Where did they all go? The exciting people doing the exciting things wearing ironical clothes? It's like I dreamt them.'

'Wait, weren't we doing the exciting things?'

'We were! Those things we did were exciting!'

'And that shirt you had was ironical.'

'Remember your ironical cardigan?'

'I do! I remember my ironical cardigan.'

'So weren't we the exciting people?'

'Yes! We were the exciting people!'

'But then.'

'Alas.'

'Look at the cut of us now.'

You sent the car careening down his shirt again and he caught it on the other end. 'Look,' he told you, reaching into my hair, 'it's in Mama's ear.' His fingers made that seashell sound as they brushed my ear and I shuddered, to be touched with such delicacy.

'Sorry, are you cold? Take my jacket.' He leaned across to drape it over my shoulders, enclosing me within the wind-break of his chest, your small body cupped in the hollow between us. You gurgled with glee. You literally gurgled.

I looked up. His honey-haired daughter was standing there. 'Hi, sweetie!' I said brightly, straightening up.

'My mummy says, em, my mummy . . . my mummy says, em . . .'

'Come here, pet,' he said, tapping his free knee, but she didn't budge, remained planted there twisting a button on her cardigan. I took you from my friend's knee and perched you on mine.

She glanced sidelong up at me, taking in her father's jacket on my shoulders. 'My mummy says, em . . . my mummy . . . em . . . says . . .'

My heart raced as I waited to hear what her mummy had to say.

'Come here, pet,' my friend instructed her again, and again she held her ground.

She sidled up to me, still holding the button on her cardi-gan. 'My mummy,' she repeated, indicating the button, and I leaned down to discover a miniature watercolour of a rabbit that I would never have noticed in a million years, it was so tiny. 'Oh look!' I exclaimed in the stupid fake voice I had already resolved not to reserve for children, 'Rabbits!'

147

'Bunnies,' she lisped softly, frowning in concentration as she rotated the button between her fingertips.

'Gosh,' I said, as much to myself as to her. Dear little things for a dear little girl. She was everywhere, my friend's tiny wife, in the big details and the small. The strapping boys she had birthed and this dainty girl. Porcelain buttons for her porcelain world.

You indicated your desire to be put down (*'Stuck!'*). The pair of you bent over the buttons, heads touching, solemnly examining them for some moments, a rabbit hole to slip down, a hidden door – like faces on patterned wallpaper or shapes in clouds: worlds no less real to a child for being imaginary.

At some signal indiscernible to us – the birds again, the flock of birds simultaneously changing direction mid-flight – the two of you pivoted and flitted away. If there was one thing I knew, it was that my friend had not picked out the cardigan studded with bunny amulets, the miraculous medals of old that mothers once sewed into their children's garments to protect them from harm.

'I'd kill for that kid,' my friend said, squinting at his daughter's receding back. 'I mean, I'd kill for any of them, but I'd really kill for her.'

I murmured assent. Her fragility weighed on me too. That was the trouble with porcelain. I sat there hunched under my friend's jacket. It was time to give it back.

* * *

148

An aside, Sailor. Some context, background, may be helpful here. I'm sorry that none of this begins with Once upon a time, like bedtime stories are meant to. When you were just a few months old, a small swaddled parcel who still fit in the pram attachment, I started those long walks around the hill. From the outside, it must have looked like I was trying to regain my figure, but I was trying to regain my mind.

You would gaze up at me during those journeys, two saucer eyes. When I smiled, you smiled back. Other times, you wondered at the sky. I felt very close to you on these walks. We were in love, you might say. It flowed between us, a particle exchange, and made me stronger, calmer, better in myself.

The road was too narrow for a footpath. An earthen verge ran along the wall. Wild flowers grew there in summer: valerian, red clover, rosebay willowherb. I'll relearn all these names and teach them to you as my father taught them to me. You can forget them too.

A man rounded the corner approaching us on the same side of the road. Late middle age, prosperous-looking, spry.

By the time he was maybe twenty feet off, it became evident that he did not intend making way for this woman and her child, that we were on a collision course. One of us was going to have to veer into the road. I gripped the pram handle with both hands. Because it wasn't going to be me. 'No, babba,' I said into the pram, 'it is not going to be me.'

At the moment before impact, although no cars were coming, he stepped not out onto the road but into the mucky bit along the wall, muttering to me as he did so.

I looked around. 'Excuse me?'

He turned and walked backwards for a few strides. 'I said: you are supposed to walk on the other side of the road.'

I rejoined with 'You can walk where you like,' or some such, I can't remember.

That's when he called me a stupid woman.

This man was dressed in a tweed jacket, mustard cords, Toad of Toad Hall. We will read that book together before too long. My father read it to me. I felt this insult like a slap on the face.

When I made it around the corner out of sight, I rang my husband and asked him what side of the road you're supposed to walk on. This was the wrong question, I see that now. My husband declared the man a dick and wanted a description. I realised that he intended jumping in the car to locate the dick and escalate the dickology. It's okay, I said. I'll be home soon.

Why am I telling you about the tweed dick all these years later? Actually, I think his jacket was waxed – I am confusing him with this other dick who wore a tweed jacket with leather elbow patches over a graph-paper shirt although he wasn't a college professor but something in property. I'll stop describing him because I'm just describing the wrong dick at this point. They all blur into one.

Conversely, although the dicks themselves blur, the nature of their dickdom is coming into sharper focus. That man saw fit to chastise me because he had never pushed a pram. He had made no contribution to the enormous effort required to raise a child and regarded me with my baby as an obstacle in his path, an obstruction to his business, which, unlike mine, was important. So he pranced around like a country squire reinforcing as best he could the ideologies of patriarchy, Empire, ideas which had held dominion for many centuries, including the one in which he and I had been born, to the extent that when he declared me a stupid woman I felt not just abused but worse: disabused – that all along I had believed I was equal, when all along I was not, because all along I had been treading towards this great crevasse called motherhood, and now that I was at the bottom of it looking up at the world through my brain fog, I could see that to have presumed Empire and patriarchy were dead was naive at best. Not only were they alive and well: they had won. Trump and Putin were in office and I became frightened of the hardness of those around me at a time when I was soft and had a baby in my care, all of which contributed to that awful day, that bad Good Friday and the fear that gripped me, which was not a fear I had experienced before, having never been weak before, nor injured, nor incompetent. I was now too stupefied to find my way back to my old life. That girl was gone and all I could do – and indeed, all I did do – was cry when you weren't looking.

I cannot say with certitude whether the encounter with the dick happened shortly before or shortly after the episode in the forest glade. It is difficult to put sequential order on a turbulent time.

Now I find I would like to know more about that dick and his impact on those in his orbit, the females in particular. Had he been more subtle, the precise nature of his dickdom would have evaded me. It can be difficult to pin down a dick, Sailor, because they shrivel away when confronted – they are dicks, after all – but sometimes, like with that big throbbing hard-on, you simply can't miss them. I was a stupid woman, yes, he had a point, but I was stupefied by the demands of caring for the next generation, by the relentless barrage of urgent tasks that eliminated the time and space to think. I am not stupid any more. But he will always be a dick.

Celandine, campion, meadowsweet, vetch. My father reciting wildflower names to his child.

I'd kill for that kid. I'd kill for any of them, but I'd really kill for her.

All the scenic children. Those happy, beautiful children. He made such wonderful children, my friend.

As did my husband.

Eyebright, tormentil, wild violet, cinquefoil. I couldn't even push a pram right. A road I had travelled all my life, a road not five minutes from the house where I'd been born, and me wondering whether I'd been walking on the wrong side all this time. A grown woman, uncertain of the ground beneath her feet. I had found myself deep in a forest, Sailor. I was lost.

Honeysuckle, loosestrife, foxglove, bracken.

I'd always thought that bracken was heather but it turns out that bracken means ferns. Bracken grew throughout the woods, edged the glade that held the hatchling.

So if you ever think I was wrong to have felt so strongly about my friend, to have taken comfort from his mere existence, I will reply that parenting is gender segregation, that I was growing progressively more alienated from the opposite sex, that my faith in masculinity was at stake and that my friend redeemed it. That in so doing he helped my marriage.

I cannot recall my riposte when that particular pillar of society pronounced me a stupid woman. My mind was no longer sharp, the way it had been before your birth. I know what I would say now: Thank you for being a dick, Dick. Were you not quite such a dick, your dickery might have flown under my radar. I have been outwitted so many times since giving birth, but unable to figure out how, and invariably my husband gets the blame. So thank you for crystallising matters, you dick. I'll be ready for you next time. And so will my son.

SIX

'Slow down, please, my neck hurts.' I put my fingertips to my glands. Two golf balls. Were they bigger than normal? I never remembered to check them when I wasn't sick so I had no baseline. 'I think I might be getting tonsillitis.'

'You're always sick.'

I frowned at my husband. What was that supposed to mean? 'If I'm always sick, it's because I never get to rest. So I never get to recover. Because you never help.'

'You never let me help.'

'Because you don't know how.'

My husband drove cars like they were motorbikes. I grappled for the handle over the door to keep myself upright as we took a corner. My phone scudded away from me across the dashboard. 'Could you slow down, please?'

'It's fine. This car has—' and he embarked on an explanation of some advanced braking feature, information that may at some point be of interest to you but, Sailor, not to me.

'Is this a hostage situation? I'm asking you to slow down. It hurts my neck when you swerve like that.' I let go of the handle to check my glands again. *Dunk*. We hit a pothole so deep it felt like a torpedo strike.

'Fuck's sake!' he yelled, veering although we'd already hit it. My phone shot past me before I could catch it, landing down the side of my door. 'Fucking state of the roads!'

'Could that give us a puncture?' I wondered. 'Should we, like, pull over and check the tyres?' He didn't pull over.

Driving changed your father's personality. You put a steering wheel into his hands and it became the steering wheel to the universe, or to something more than a car anyway. The problem with the universe was that it was full of cretins and his wheel didn't control their cars.

'Slug! Where's the funeral?

'Heap of scrap!

'Organ donor!'

'They can't hear you,' I pointed out. 'You know that, right? That they can't hear you?

'It's just that,' I continued when he didn't respond, 'you keep trying to engage with them as if they can hear you.'

I shrugged. 'I'm sitting right here and you could alternatively talk to me? Your wife?'

'We're late,' he said tightly.

I turned the temperature dial to red.

He turned it back to blue. 'It's too hot.'

'Take off your coat.'

'I can't. I'm driving.'

I twisted around to look at you in the back seat, the big yellow S on your Superman top. You seemed warm enough.

Micra up ahead, red rag to a bull. The bull slowed down to Micra speed and locked onto the red rag's bumper. A silent tension gripped the car. There is always a possibility when your father overtakes that we are all going to die.

A gap in the oncoming traffic. I was thrust sideways as he accelerated into the opposite lane. He leaned forward to peer at the Micra driver as we sped past, for the steering wheel that crowned him king revealed the decrepitude of others. The Steering Wheel of Truth. I don't know much about cars, Sailor, but I know they had a physical effect on that man. The electromagnetic waves or whatever travelled up the steering column and infused his cells, enhancing his superiority while pronouncing the failings of others.

He pulled back onto the correct side of the road and I found myself jabbering in relief. 'It always feels like you're trespassing when you're speeding on the wrong side of the road, doesn't it? Kind of like you're a burglar and you might get caught. And now it's like, woo, we got away with it! Do you know what I mean?'

'Nope.'

Yep, got it: we were late. And it was my fault. But was it my fault? He certainly thought so. He had been ready all morning, performatively waiting while I got you ready. Patiently watching TV. Watching football, which was worse. By the time I had you ready, there was no time left for me to get ready. I'd chucked my make-up bag into the glovebox.

'It's twenty past eleven,' he had informed me.

'I am aware of that,' I had informed him back, trying to balance the towel on my head as I rushed around, late out of the shower because you wouldn't eat your breakfast. 'You could help?' I had suggested. 'You could get off the couch and pack the nappy bag?'

'With what?'

'The stuff he needs.'

'What does he need?'

'His *stuff*,' I had repeated by way of explanation. 'The stuff. You know, all the stuff.' But my husband didn't know all the stuff. How would he? Stuff was for the little people. The soother, the spare soother, the nappies, the wipes, the barrier cream, change of clothes, Calpol, a snack, a spare snack for when the first snack was rejected. I'd tried to say the words but there were just so many of them that it'd be quicker to pack the bag myself. 'It's okay,' I had sighed like my mother had sighed before me and hers before her as I headed upstairs to your bedroom.

'We're getting *later*,' he had called up from the couch.

'I *know*,' I had called down from your room. A teddy. A handful of little cars. No doubt the wrong little cars, no doubt the wrong teddy, but anyway, anyway.

'Don't forget the wine,' he'd said without looking up from the screen when I'd reappeared in the living room with dry hair and the bag of stuff. The roar of the crowd in the stadium, a sound that manages to be simultaneously inane and intimidating. Maybe one day you'll explain the male mind to me, Sailor. Women don't gather in hordes to hurl abuse at individuals doing an infinitely better job than they ever could.

I'd grabbed a bottle from the rack and put it in his hand.

He'd frowned at the label. 'You're not bringing that one, are you?'

I'd swopped it for another on the rack. All wine bottles look the same to me, Sailor, especially when I'm late. There are red bottles and there are white bottles. Some people – generally male people – have the time to study the difference between the two.

I'd handed him the new bottle. 'Acceptable?'

He'd looked at the label then up at me. 'You look great. Have we a bag or something for this?' He'd switched off the TV and headed out to wait in the car.

I turned to you. 'Okay,' I said in my fake bright voice, 'let's go!' Off you ran, the Superman cape flowing in your wake. Off I ran after you. Keystone Cops.

The front door opened after some minutes. 'What's the delay?'

'I can't catch him.'

'Do as your mother says!' your father bellowed so loudly that you burst into tears.

'Stop,' I said, 'he isn't well.'

'See? You always undermine me.'

'You gave him his medicine, right?' You had tonsillitis again. Or had had it. You were over it but the course of anti-biotics had to be finished.

'No.'

'Why not?'

'I forgot.'

'But we agreed that would be your job. Like, your one and only job.'

'And I'm sorry. I forgot.'

159

I opened the fridge to get your medicine and found last night's syringe still full. I held it up. 'Last night's dose is still here.'

'Shit,' he said, 'sorry.'

'I even measured it out for you.'

'I know. Shit. I'm sorry.'

'There's no point in apologising to me. It's not me you're harming.'

'Oh, I'm harming my child now?'

'You can't just stop a course of antibiotics.'

'Look at him. He's fine.' And to demonstrate your fineness, you shot past with a speed that was impressive, even for you. You had seen the medicine.

'Yucky!' you yelled from under the kitchen table. 'No!'

'I'll wait in the car,' my husband told me and headed for the door.

'Thanks for the help,' I said to his back.

'No!' you yelled.

I put my head in my hands. I don't think I'd put my head in my hands – actually lowered my head into my open hands expressly to block out the sight of the world – until I had you. And then – after the protracted negotiations and laborious palaver of getting you medicated, shod, out the door and into the car seat, making us a whole forty minutes late – a heart-sinking stink reached my nose.

I took you back up. 'He needs a nappy change.'

To which your father said nothing. It was the way he said it, though.

* * *

'Why do they have to make these things so tricky?' I muttered as I always muttered when failing the car-seat buckle aptitude test. 'Do they really have to make them so difficult?'

'Right,' said my husband from the front seat. 'The car-seat industry is a big conspiracy to make women look stupid.' Oh yes, we were very, very late.

I got the two metal inserts of the buckle to connect, then you arched your back and busted them apart before I could locate the socket in which to slot them. It was dangling in the footwell. I pressed your wriggling body down with my forearm, got the two halves together again and pushed them into the socket as hard as I could. Wouldn't go. Maybe the socket needed oil. Did plastic need oil? The inserts finally clicked into position, catching the side of my finger. 'Ow!' I yelped.

I got into the front seat nursing my finger. Blood blister. I wanted my husband to ask if I was alright, cross with myself for wanting his attention. He knew I wanted it. But he withheld it. Because we were late, late!

He put the key in the ignition and the radio blared at full volume. 'What the—' He pulled out the key.

'Oh,' I said. 'He was playing with the car yesterday.'

'You let him play with the car?'

'I had to.'

'You had to?'

'It rained all day. I ran out of things to do.'

'The car is not a toy.'

'Really? I thought the car *was* a toy. Thanks for clearing

that up. Christ, I was such a fucking moron before I met you.'

'Try not to curse in front of the child.'

'Oh gosh, another great parenting tip from the expert.' And so on and so forth. I don't have to tell you. You were there. Hostage situation.

My husband rotated the stereo dial until it clicked off before returning the key to the ignition. *Rrrrrr, rrrrrr, rrrrrr* as the engine struggled to catch. My husband glanced down at the lighting stem. 'The lights were left on overnight,' he pointed out, and switched them off. *Rrrrr, rrrrrr, rrrrrr*, the sound of our failing spirits. One last time pumping the accelerator, then he placed his forehead on the steering wheel. The three of us sat in silence on the driveway for some moments. Then my husband got out of the car, slammed the door and walked away.

I thought he was going to keep walking, that that was it, we were done. A car is not a toy. Nor is a marriage. Alright, I thought, I can deal with this. I turned around to look at you. 'Good boy,' I said. 'It's okay.' But it wasn't. Panic, real fear, was rising up my throat. 'This isn't fun any more,' he had said the night before, meaning our life together. Then the door opened again and my husband reached in to pop a lever, a set of jump leads under his arm. He reappeared in the front windscreen and raised the bonnet, erecting a sheet of metal between us.

I examined my blood blister. This is how marriages fall apart, Sailor. Not over infidelity or even lack of love, but over batteries, antibiotics, car seats.

* * *

My husband viewed our Prius as a chemical castration, a punishment I had levied on him by endlessly pointing out the challenges of loading a baby into the back seat of his three-door coupe. He was driving too closely to the car in front. 'You're driving too closely to the car in front,' I said.

'I can stop faster than he can.'

'I'd like to be able to see its wheels, that's all. We're so close that I can't see its back wheels.'

'It's fine.' That word again.

'How do you *know?*' I asked. 'How do you *know* whether you can stop faster than the driver in front? Have you tried it out? Did the pair of you meet up somewhere, like on some abandoned road, and say, alright bud, on the count of three, let's see who can stop faster?'

My husband didn't respond.

'Because if you're wrong – and obviously you are never wrong – but if you are, it's the life of your wife and child that's at stake.'

He still didn't leave a safe stopping distance.

I turned to look at him, at the side of his head. 'What makes you so confident?' I asked, genuinely curious. 'How come I go around knowing that I know nothing, but you are certain of uncertainties, like whether you can brake faster than a complete stranger?'

'This car brakes faster than that car. That's engineering.'

'Engineering? Oh well, *then*.'

'I am an excellent driver.'

'You are a skilled driver, but not a safe one.'

He slowed down to create a safe stopping distance. 'Ring ahead. Tell them we are going to be extremely late.'

I searched my bag. 'My phone isn't here. I must have left it at home.'

'It fell off the dashboard.'

'Oh yeah.' I located it wedged down the side of my seat but my hand didn't fit in the gap. 'Can't get at it,' I said flatly.

'Use mine.' He released it from the dashboard mount.

But his was an iPhone and I was used to Android. I prodded inanely at the screen. There was a time when I could have figured it out, when I possessed a mind that was fluid and focused and able to solve problems. Like, how to make a call from a phone.

'Forget it,' my husband said when I started cursing the bloody thing. He took it out of my hand.

In the event of an accident, read the insurance disc holder, do not admit liability. 'If you didn't drive like a maniac, then my phone would not be jammed down the side of the seat.'

'If you were on time, then I would not drive like a maniac.'

'If you helped with our child, then I would be on time.'

'If you *let* me help with our child, then I would help with our child.'

'If you could be trusted to help with our child, then I would *let* you help with our child. You didn't even give him his medicine.'

And so on for miles. If you this, then I that. The street sign said yield, but I wouldn't. The next one said stop, but

I couldn't. Nor could your father. The pair of us bickering about you as if you weren't there. My husband was his most concentrated self when enclosed in a car. And I was my most concentrated self too, strapped in beside him. Shame our most concentrated selves were our worst ones.

The road split into two lanes. He moved into the outer lane and flashed his headlamps at the driver ahead. When the driver didn't pull in, he swerved into the inner lane and over-took the car that way, or undertook it, swerving back into the outer lane as soon as he had gotten ahead. 'We're making good time,' he remarked.

A brand new white Range Rover pulled out onto the road, or maybe it was a Land Rover. The distinction was crucial but I could never remember it. One was the hallmark of a dick, according to the Steering Wheel of Truth.

The lights up ahead turned red. I flipped down the vanity mirror and unscrewed the top of my mascara.

My husband pulled up alongside the SUV. It was taller than our car, so tall that when I glanced out my side window all I saw was door. 'Tell me when the lights change,' I mur-mured, easing the mascara wand through my lashes.

When two men stop at traffic lights there can only be one winner. 'Changed,' said my husband, abruptly flooring it and throwing me backwards. The SUV caught up with us and we travelled neck and neck at motorway speed along the resi-dential road.

'I am your wife!' I found myself shouting, jamming my foot down where the brake pedal should be, this white tank inches to my left. 'I am your wife! I am your wife!' We entered a roundabout locked together like synchronised swimmers – no, like synchronised dicks – the wine bottle clunking under my seat, then clunking the other side when we exited. *'I am your wife!'* We raced along until a car up ahead turning right blocked our passage. My husband braked hard before veering into the inner lane, tucking us in tightly behind the SUV, the tailgate of which reared up in our windscreen. 'Guh!' I cried in fright, raising my arms to shield myself.

He let the SUV accelerate away and put his hand on mine. 'I'm sorry.'

'Keep your hands on the wheel.'

He returned his hand to the wheel. 'I'm sorry,' he said again.

I twisted around to look at you. You stared back with worried eyes, Superman sucking a soother. Everything about you makes me want to cry.

* * *

Motorway. Industrial buildings, parking lots, power lines. Nothing was familiar, neither the landscape outside nor the man by my side. And I was clearly a stranger to him. More than I had understood. I am your wife, I had found myself yelling. By which I meant: that man in the SUV? You do not know that man. You do not live with that man. That man does not cook your meals or wash your clothes or raise your child. He does not share your bed. You would not recognise that man on the street. That man may not even be a man for all you know. That man may be a woman. Or a drug dealer with a gun in his glovebox. Why have you entered into a relationship that can only be described as personal with that man? To the detriment of your family? My focus had honed in on the occupants of the car, particularly the one in the back seat, like those metaphysical lovers who made one little room an everywhere. An equivalent adjustment had not taken place in my husband's world. His world in fact largely excluded us. You've changed, was the other thing he had said the night before. Trouble was, he hadn't.

I put my hand on the window. Fatalistic pronouncements were coming at me like traffic.

We have nothing left to lose. It has already been lost.

He hardly notices we're here. He'll hardly notice we're gone.

On some fundamental level, we already are gone.

These were the private thoughts I was harbouring in my heart.

A man comes home late from work on Good Friday after an ugly fight with his wife. Ugly ugly ugly, the worst they've ever known. Barely recognised one another. Unplumbed reservoirs of hate. She hasn't been taking his calls all day. Those things he said after she hit him. Well well well. She knows he doesn't mean them, right? It's the Easter break. They were supposed to go away but he went to the office. Maybe they can go to the hotel tomorrow instead? The house is in darkness. The car is missing. Other stuff too if he cared to look. He turns on the hall light, walks down the corridor. The bouncer chair is mangled. Looks like someone jumped on it. He pushes open the living room door, dread rising. She is sitting on the floor in front of the fire with their baby. Relief but also alarm. Why is she huddled in the dark? He turns on the light and she winces at the brightness so he switches it back off but he has seen it, her face. Her eyeliner, her mascara or whatever it's called, streaks her cheeks black. Like Joker in *Batman*, he thinks, but manages not to say this out loud. He approaches and peers at her in the firelight. Is that blood? My God, what happened to your face? A crown of thorns for the day that's in it. Their child is not scratched. Look at him, oh my God, perfect. Mother and baby did not follow the same trajectory that day. He asks her if she's okay. She says she's fine. She says everything is *fine*, her code red word. And he goes, Ah great, that's grand, your cardigan's on inside out, silly thing, what's for dinner?

Like: come on, you know? *Come on.*

'What's that?' my husband asked.

I turned to look at him. 'Nothing.'

We eventually left the motorway and reached that road with the high stone wall running along one side. What was behind it? Hospital? School? One of those religious institutions locking children away from love? Or their broken mothers. 'See this bend coming up?' my husband said. 'I once took it at over a hundred miles an hour. Got my knee right down.' He smiled at the memory. Back when his life was brilliant. It was miraculous he had survived to pass on his DNA.

'You've gone very quiet,' he observed when I made no comment.

I glanced into the back seat. You had drifted off. 'I don't know what to say to you any more.'

'That doesn't sound good.'

'It isn't.'

I had followed him around the house one time. You were just a tiny baby in my arms and I had wanted to know who he would save if there was a fire and he could only save one of us. I would save you both, was his answer. '*No*,' I corrected him because he wasn't grasping the premise, 'you can only save one of us and it has to be our baby. If I could only save one of us,' I told him, 'it would have to be our baby, and you would have to save him too.'

'I would save you both,' he repeated. 'I don't like this question.'

I didn't like the question either because I knew I would leave my husband behind in the fire, I would leave him to burn, oh I would leave my poor love to burn, and leave myself to burn with him if need be.

My question wasn't a question, I see now, but an acknowledgement of the brutal but necessary displacement that had taken place with your arrival. Bullet points, Sailor. I am tired tonight, and it was all just bullets and points when you were small, shooting them and scoring them and who knew it was going to descend into that? We had the best of intentions, your father and I, when we started a family. We had love, so much love. We wanted to share it. To articulate it, allow it to

169

manifest, our bounty. We spilled over with love. And then we just spilled it. You will never know how happy your parents were. We had become just another warring couple. I looked up to see a plane crossing the blue sky and wanted to be on it. Didn't care where it was going. That plane was going away. I wanted to go there too.

My husband left the road with the stone wall and drove past a church, a small graveyard, oblivious to the enmity brewing beside him. He was still playing racing cars, like your cars only bigger, more dangerous. He did not understand where the real threat lay. Not with other drivers but his passenger. I felt a burst of pity for him then. 'I don't like you when you drive,' I tried as a way of alerting him.

'But we were late. And now we're less late.' Brightly, as if he'd solved a problem. Unaware, evidently, that there was a bigger problem.

'No, I mean, I *really* don't like you. I don't think you understand how little I like you when you drive.'

Trees, a row of shops. Kids kicking a ball.

'Otherwise you wouldn't drive this way,' I added, but he wasn't getting it. I checked that you were still napping. 'Remember when he was a few weeks old and you got a bad cold? You sent me this text from bed asking for soup and I hated you. I was downstairs crying and bleeding and lactating and I got that text and I hated you.'

'Why would you hate me? I had flu.'

'You had a cold. I'd had surgery.'

'Why are you bringing this up now?'

170

'I'm explaining.'

'Explaining what?'

'How easy it was to hate you. Maybe it was just resentment but it felt like hate.'

'Hate's a strong word. I would hate for you to hate me. I'm sorry that I frightened you earlier.'

'It's not just the driving, it's everything. The way you have abandoned me.'

'I haven't abandoned you. I would never abandon you.'

'I'm trying to tell you something here. I'm trying to warn you, out of the love that I had for you.'

'Had?'

'I still love you.'

'Still?'

'Do you still love me?'

'Of course. I never stopped. I never could stop. How can you ask?'

He took another right. We were running out of time. 'Where is this going?'

'Dundrum.'

'Our marriage. Where is it going?'

'What do you mean? I just got a promotion.'

'How could you not get a promotion?'

'You mean congratulations?'

'No, I mean, how could you *not* get a promotion when you're always at the office? You've a wife who does all the cooking, cleaning and child-rearing. She pairs your socks, she books your dental appointments. She sorts out all this shit,' I said, tapping the tax and insurance discs displayed on the windscreen. 'I've no time for my career, but you've more time for yours than you did before becoming a father, back when we were equal.'

'We are equal. We're a team.'

'We're not a team. The lot of you in there discussing your wives' post-natal depression over the water cooler so you can feel like concerned husbands. All you need to do is help. But instead, you work late. You stay in the office until you're sure all the babies have gone to bed. Then you congratulate yourselves on how hard you're working. Your bosses promote you for shirking family responsibilities while your wives' careers dwindle to a halt because somebody is left holding the baby. And our child's going to grow up to think I'm a nag, same as I grew up thinking my mother was a nag, because it would be so much easier if the mothers shut up and did everything without perennially protesting about it.'

'That's not fair.'

'What's the point?' I continued, ignoring him. 'If I'm this unhappy, what's the point?'

'You're unhappy?'

'Yes! Aren't you?'

'No. I'm very happy.'

'Well, of course you are. You've won.'

'I want you to be happy too. I can ask my mother to help.'

'Why can't you help? Why is the duty of care entirely on me? When did everything get so fucked up?'

'What are these questions? Where are they coming from?

172

I don't know what's happening.' He glanced across at me in alarm. 'Is something happening? Are we in trouble? Tell me.'

'Green van,' you announced out of nowhere.

'Good boy!' we proclaimed in unison.

* * *

He pulled into the driveway, shut off the engine, licked his thumb and rubbed at my eyebrow. 'Mascara,' he said, 'sorry.' Then he took my hand. 'I love you.'

He waited for me to reciprocate but I just sat there looking at him. Sometimes it's unnerving, how alike you and he are. I thought of my friend then. I didn't want my friend to be my husband. I wanted my husband to be my friend.

The front door opened. His mother came out. One minute he is the man steering the universe, the next my husband is a spurned child. Specifically, this woman's spurned child. She made her way down the driveway, beamed at her boy and threw her arms wide. 'Darling!' she cried.

SEVEN

Your digitised shriek on the monitor jolted me out of bed. *Jesus Christ* from my husband's side when I knocked over the bedside lamp. I hadn't made the decision to run – it was a thing that was happening to me. 'It's okay,' I called as I blundered through the darkness. 'It's alright, darling. I'm coming.'

A blow to my shoulder. The doorframe, knocking a curse out of me as it knocked me off course.

You'd been sleeping through the night the past few months but there you were, holding onto the safety rail and howling. All the audio-activated devices were on the go – the star projector, the lullaby machine, that green singing dog. The room whirled like a poltergeist. You howled louder when you saw me.

'Turn that thing off!' my husband yelled from our bedroom.

'He's a *child*,' I yelled back.

'The monitor! Turn it off!'

I glanced around the spinning room. You were shrieking at that pitch that scrambles the brain signals. Where was the monitor? The searchlights of your star machine swept over the blank faces of the teddy bears. 'I can't find it!'

'Pull the plug out!'

'You pull it out!' Pleased with myself. The monitor was, after all, plugged in on his side too.

I turned my attention to you. 'Now.' An acrid stink. You had never smelled like that before. Your hands stretched towards my neck as mine closed around your ribs. And then your small body was clambering into mine and we were doing our thing, exchanging photons, or protons, getting our hit.

Your skin blazed against mine. I switched off the lullaby machine and we swayed to the singing dog. 'Dear oh dear,' I crooned, putting my hand to your hot forehead. 'Dear oh dear oh dear.'

The neck of your babygrow was wet. I sniffed it. That was the source of the smell. Acidic drool gone stale. Your whole front, in fact, was wet. You were teething again.

'Dear oh dear. Let's get you changed.'

I carried you into the bathroom and switched on the light. You winced and started crying again. Your cheeks were mottled in a raised scarlet rash. 'Close the door!' from the bedroom. 'I've an early start!'

I slammed the bathroom door hard because that's how articulate I was back then. You don't need a dick to be one. Though it helps. The bang made you cry harder. 'Oh poor darling, let's take your temperature.' Your arms and legs tightened around me when I tried to put you on the change table as if I were lowering you into a bubbling cauldron.

I took down the thermometer and inserted the nozzle into your ear as best as I was able while holding you to my hip. *Beep beep beep:* the fever alert. 39.1. How bad was that? I needed to google it. My phone was in the angry bear's lair. You batted me away as I tried to get the nozzle into your other ear. *Beep beep beep.* 38.9. I flicked the lid of the Calpol box open with my free hand. There was no syringe inside. It was in the dishwasher.

'Shush now,' I murmured as we ventured back out onto the landing, 'we don't want to wake Dadda now, do we?' But apparently we did and he duly roused himself up onto his hind legs to shut the bedroom door. We made our way down the stairs. The darkness calmed you, or maybe it cowed you because you fell quiet. You had never seen the house this way: the fire dead in the grate, the table lamps extinguished. The place looked barren when I switched on the overhead lights. Have you ever seen a nightclub with the lights up? Because that's what the house looked like: something you have never seen. It's all a big scam, Sailor. Cosiness, glamour, atmosphere in general – it's all just a trick of the light. One you need to master.

The dishwasher hadn't finished its cycle. Meaning it wasn't as late as I had thought. I glanced at the kitchen clock but registered little more than that there was a kitchen clock.

I tried to put you down but you clung on tighter and started grizzling again, your forehead a hot cannonball pushing into my neck. I clamped you to me with one hand and pulled down the dishwasher door with the other. The motor cut off and with it your tears. The washing machine had a porthole so you could see what was going on inside, but the inner workings of the dishwasher? You knew an opportunity when you saw one. A theatrical *whoof* of steam cleared to reveal a dripping metal maw, like part of a ship winched from the

177

seabed. You relinquished my neck to get a better look.

I pulled out the bottom drawer and removed the cutlery caddy, fished around for the syringe. 'Soothy!' you cried, diving on your soother. I intervened before you got it in your mouth.

'It's dirty. Yuck.'

A howl like a blast from a furnace.

'Jesus, okay.' Dishwasher juice was trapped in the hollow yellowing teat. You sampled it like a sommelier.

Back upstairs to the change table. Christ, that rash. I reached for the Calpol.

The syringe. It was still downstairs. 'Fuck.'

'Fuck,' you said.

'Bother.'

'Fuck,' you said. Down in the kitchen I had no idea why my head was back in the dishwasher. Something to do with the cutlery caddy? Just a bunch of knives and forks. I closed my eyes and trawled the blackness, casting my mind out like a fishing line. 'Why am I standing here?' I asked myself out loud. 'What did I come here for?'

Purple. 'The Calpol syringe!' It was on the draining board. I grabbed it and carted you up the stairs again. Oh, you were a pitiful mewling creature, sobbing with the soother clenched between your teeth like a cigar.

I needed both hands to suck the syrup into the syringe but you would not be put down. So I placed your bottom on the change table and, with your hands still padlocked around my neck, filled the syringe behind your back. I snatched the soother out of your mouth, poked the syringe into the gap and emptied the barrel. You released my neck to push me away. 'Good boy,' I coached you, rubbing your back to ease the passage of the syrup. Gloopy liquid exuded from your lips like milk boiling over. I grabbed the towel.

I refilled the syringe and tried again with the same result, except this time you ejected it forcefully. It was my face I had to wipe, not yours. And then you started to cry again, sitting there forlornly, your hair fever-damp, your cheeks blotched scarlet. Hot sticky tears and cold sticky syrup trickled down your face. Your lips, red and swollen, were more beautiful than ever.

'I think I can see a new tooth!' I exclaimed in my children's-TV-presenter voice. 'Can I have a look?' I ran my index finger over your back gums. You clamped down hard and I yelped. At which you blinked in fright before screaming at full belt. It was over. Any further attempt to medicate you would be met with maximum resistance. I tried to take your temperature again but you slapped me away.

Just make him take the medicine, my husband's internalised voice instructed me. He is the child. You are the adult. Just make him take it. Jesus.

'You need to take the medicine,' I explained as much to myself as to you. 'That's all there is to it. It has to be done. So be the best boy for me, okay? Be the best boy, please?'

We do not negotiate with terrorists, I heard my husband say. How much easier being the general in command headquarters than the soldier in the trenches. Just because I am unable to make this point cogently, Sailor, does not mean it isn't an important one.

I took down a different box, Nurofen this time. 'Look, it's the yummy orange one!' I filled the syringe and pumped the syrup into your mouth. You expunged it down your front.

Your baby has a fever, my husband stated. Medicate your baby. How hard can it be?

Back to the medicine cabinet. There was a sachet of homeopathic teething crystals. They're bullshit, my husband said. You are an intelligent woman. I cannot believe you fell for that overpriced bullshit. Nor could I. I knew they were bullshit. But I was buying something else: a last straw, a no stone left unturned, an I'll try anything at this stage, whatever it takes, I just want to stop the tears. I sprinkled the crystals into your mouth and you stopped crying to taste them. It's just sugar, expensive sugar, your father sighed, shaking his head. Because he is not the one on the front line. People go to seances, Sailor, if they are desperate enough. Human behaviour is dictated by need, not logic.

As soon as the crystals dissolved, you started sobbing again. The rash was spreading and you were crying, looking to me for help.

I rifled through the cabinet and found a box of paracetamol baby suppositories that I had quite forgotten about. I gasped when I took off your nappy. Your poor little bottom was raw. Which meant your insides were burning, your cheeks were burning, your head was burning, and your gums. Everything was burning yet you wouldn't take the medicine.

You wouldn't take the simple measure that would improve everything, opting instead to make things hard on yourself. You are indeed my son.

I apologised as I inserted the slim white bullet and you screeched in protest. The drool had soaked through your babygrow to your vest. I unpeeled the wet cotton to discover a spray of speckled bumps across your chest. They hadn't been there that morning. They hadn't been there before bed. I put on a new nappy then swept my hair along your bare skin, weaving slowly up and down from your head to your toes. The sobbing gave way as you reached your hands up into it. You didn't grab it, just let it flow through your fingers. Back and forth I wove until we were both calm. Then I dressed you in a fresh vest and picked you up. Your cheeks were still hot but the tears had at last stopped.

Then the tears came again and with them a smell. I tied up my hair and undid your poppers. Diarrhoea. Which was exactly what had happened last time I'd given you a suppository. Which was why, indeed, I'd stopped giving you suppositories. There's a Bowie song, *Always Crashing in the Same Car*. It's about someone who keeps making the same mistake. Like triggering diarrhoea by inserting a suppository, except it's about something epic, a grand emotion. I had thought motherhood would involve telling you about David Bowie, passing my knowledge on like a key to the world. The suppository hadn't been in long enough to offer relief. Sorry, sorry, sorry, I murmured as I cleaned you up. The wipe was stinging your skin.

You were too hot so I didn't dress you. You looked so cute in your nappy but you were bewildered and exhausted by the pain. I took your temperature again. 40.2. Crunch time. I filled up the Nurofen syringe and cupped the back of your head. 'I'm sorry, you just have to swallow this. That's all there is to it.' I wormed the syringe into the corner of your mouth and squirted.

You convulsed, gagging in silence as if your airways were sealed. We stared at each other in panic. 'Oh honey,' I said, and clasped your shoulders. A ripple ran through your body, then you vomited the syrup out along with a pungent bile. This wasn't one of your usual milky barfs. It was stringy and clotted, like egg white, and it kept coming until it was streaming out of your nostrils. You wailed pleadingly up at me, the murder weapon still in my hand. I needed to google your symptoms. But my phone was still in the bedroom.

I plonked you into the empty bath for safekeeping and ran as fast as I could into the bedroom. *Shut up*, I was ready to bellow if my husband objected, but all he did was raise his head from the pillow and drop it again. I unplugged my phone and returned to find you bawling and slathered in more vomit.

Vomiting toddler temperature over 40, I googled while you implored me to lift you out of the bath. 'Just a minute.' A load of chatrooms of other mothers asking what to do if their vomiting LO's temperatures were over 40, but no clear diagnosis. Just mothers sympathising with other mothers, mothers offering helpful suggestions. Mothers, mothers,

mothers, pink garters, doing their best. I leaned into the bath to kiss the top of your head, the only part of you that was clean. 'Oh poor darling, let's get you sorted.' I sponged the vomit off you, towelled the puddle off the floor and dressed you in fresh cotton. And then you were clean and we were in one another's arms again and it took a while but eventually your sobs ebbed and you forgave me.

'Will we shine the torch?' I asked and you brightened. Anything involving the phone was a welcome development. I laid you back down on the change table gurning at you as if it were all a great lark and asked you to open your mouth.

There was some class of blister on the ridge of gum at the back. It was small and rubbery and translucent, like a fish's egg.

'Oh, poor darling. I see the problem.' I googled *toddler gums absess*.

Do you mean abscess? the phone asked.

That's when you did the scream. You hit this note that ricocheted around the tiled walls so that it was coming at me from every angle. I didn't know what to do and turned one way then the other. Had the abscess burst? Would that poison the blood? Is that what this fever was? Sepsis? 'I'm trying to sleep!' your father yelled from the bedroom.

It was the powerlessness that was so frightening. The middle of the night and my child was in crisis. There was no one I could run it past to check it was okay, it was normal, that there was nothing to worry about.

The health insurance doctor line.

I googled the number, you wailing the whole time because I was ignoring you.

'Perfect,' said the person on the other end of the line when I gave my name, as if a name could be perfect. 'And your membership number?'

'I don't know,' I said over your screams.

I described your symptoms: vomiting, diarrhoea, rashes, fever, small hard spherical abscessy *thing* where a molar may be coming up. Yeah, the rash is kind of raised, I said in answer to her question. I stretched it with my fingers to see if it would blanch. Yes, it blanches, I confirmed. No, his breathing seems to be fine. Yes, he's alert. No, no fits. Well, he sort of convulsed before he vomited. Convulsed, she repeated. I needed someone to tell me it wasn't anything sinister. In case it was something sinister. You hear stories. Sailor, you hear the saddest of stories.

The woman told me to keep you cool and to offer you water. Well, she told me to give you paracetamol but I laughed grimly. She said that if at any point you went limp or unresponsive, I was to take you straight to A&E. She advised me that a doctor would ring back in an hour. I'd thought she was the doctor.

I picked up the thermometer but you'd had enough of it by then. I didn't need a thermometer to tell me you were on fire. I gathered you up and carried you out to the landing. The bedroom door opened when I was halfway down the stairs. 'Please,' my husband said over your grizzling, 'I have a big day tomorrow. Is he okay?'

'He's *fine*.'

My husband nodded and closed the door and I resented him then as I had never resented anyone in my life. And I resented resenting him because I had never been a resentful woman until he got all the freedom and I got all the resentment. He had a big day ahead but I only had little days. This was merely *teething trouble* – a deliberate use of understatement to trivialise conditions men don't have to bother with.

'Come on,' I said, 'let's get you a cool drink.'

But oh you did not want a cool drink. You did not want your soother. You did not want a moist cloth on your forehead or to peer into the dishwasher. You did not want to be put down but did not want to be held either. How you cried. How you burned. Oh gosh how you burned, and oh gosh how I panicked, as if there were a finite amount of you which would burn up altogether, leaving behind a small heap of ash. Around the kitchen I paced with you crying in my arms. A whole hour until the doctor rang!

I put you in the buggy and pulled a coat over my pyjamas, runners onto my feet.

You stopped crying once we ventured out into the darkness as if light had been the problem, as if it had been burning you, giving you sunstroke, whatever sunstroke is. I never knew how much could go wrong with the human body until I became responsible for your one.

You were solemn but wide awake as we progressed up the road. Not a soul about. Should have switched on the television to get the painkillers in, I realised as I pushed the buggy towards the harbour. Or handed you the phone. Screens turned you into a zombie. I could have stuck pins in you so long as you had a screen. All the things I should have done. I could fill a baby manual with them. Another baby manual that no man would ever read, just mothers, tired, bewildered mothers who would think: *hey, that'll work!* and then instantly forget it because it is so hard to think straight when someone is screaming in your face.

'Yes, it is,' I said into the buggy. 'It is so hard to think straight.' I want to be the one to tell you about David Bowie but I won't get to be the one because I don't get to think straight. Someday, before too long, your father will put down his newspaper and take you aside, just as his father put down his newspaper and took him aside, namely because he could, namely because he had the time to look up from his newspaper – to even have a newspaper – and then impart his world view. And I'll be . . . I don't know, restocking bog-roll holders or googling *leftover roast chicken recipes* or pairing little boy socks. Pairing big man socks. I put my palm on your forehead. It did seem a bit cooler. I touched your cheeks. Definitely cooler. Relief.

And quiet, how quiet you were, so quiet that I could think. You've no idea what your screams did to me, Sailor. I've no idea what they did either. They shook my brain, flung it in whirling fragments like the contents of a snow globe. But as we walked, the spinning particles drifted back to earth to form a layer, acquiring cohesion once more, concord, an explosion in reverse. Step by step, street by street, my mind softly returned to itself. It came to rest on the surfaces around us, concealing the disarray, tamping down the chaos, and I pushed you through a new landscape, which was, I suppose, the old landscape, that of my own head before it was scattered to the four winds, a mind of winter I barely recognised, I had been away that long. Like growing back an amputated limb. Something you thought was gone – something in fact that you had forgotten you even had, you had hobbled around without it for so long – but which, now that you have been gifted it back, you realise was the quality, the essence, that thing, that maddening *thing*, that has been missing all this time.

You think you know me. How can you know me? This isn't me.

At the zebra crossing you abruptly lurched toward the button although there wasn't any traffic. 'Good boy!' I exclaimed at this evidence of recovery. I angled the buggy up on two wheels so you could reach the large disk, but you didn't press hard enough so I went to do it. 'No, I!' you objected, pulling my hand away to press the button again yourself, again not hard enough, so I took your hand and, as if fingerprinting you, pushed your digits against the button because that's how long it takes to get from A to B with a small child in tow. There is a reason why mothers look so slow and plodding as we lumber about. I set the buggy back down on four wheels and we waited. The lights turned orange, then red, and the invisible traffic stopped. The green man appeared and we were off.

We crossed to the sea wall. It was a clear night, very beautiful, very still – you will not remember it. I took a photo to file away for the auditor who will one day decree whether I gave you a happy childhood or not, but it came out black. I like to think the image is tucked away in your mind, though, informing the man you will one day become. This is what I like to think: that it's all there, or not all of it, just the good stuff – the midsummer stars as keen as anything, the moon gilding the waves silver, the horizon a dark expanse, the world before man. The lack of bearings took down my fever too, Sailor, which was a different type of fever altogether, a fever which on one level I hope you don't inherit, and on another I pray you do, it being the fever that makes life interesting. I felt good, little Sailor. I felt like myself. I started singing to you, not because I can sing, but despite the fact that I can't.

We were down on the lower path by then because I had turned the buggy around on a whim and veered away from the world of electric light. It was a place I would never ordinarily venture at night, being out of sight from the main road and therefore unsafe for lone women because . . . you don't need to know. But it was two or three o'clock in the morning and who else was going to be out at that hour? Only the mothers of other feverish infants. Tiny women trapped in snow globes pushing tiny prams through sleeping towns, fragments of our fractured minds tinkling like shrapnel around us.

You thinking your thoughts, me thinking mine. It occurred to me that when the day came for you to consider your mother objectively, you would perceive in her the limitations of your destiny. If all you saw, day in, day out, was this woman who couldn't finish sentences or remember to pack the wipes, and who forgot items on the shopping list even though they were written down, forgot the shopping list itself, and who was tired, so tired, and who complained of that tiredness relentlessly until it became a background drone that no one really heard any more, like traffic, it would weigh down your conception of yourself and of who you could be. It would circumscribe any young man's ambition, wouldn't it? Duty compelled me to illustrate that the drudge before you was not your mother, as such, that I owed it to you to show you who you really were by showing you who I really was. Does that make sense? It did at the time. Under the stars that night, surrounded by a vertiginous infinity of sea and sky, having fallen through a pocket in time, or out of time, when everyone slept except my child and me, this made sense. I try so hard to beat carrots and peas into you but there is so much more, Sailor, that I want to shove down your throat. These were the thoughts I was thinking when I noticed the shape up ahead, lurking in the lee of the lifeguard's hut.

There is a thing that happens to a woman when she is alone in the dark – shall I lay this out for you now? Explain about the curfew? How in the darkness, women become prey. Captured in their snow globes. A hyper alertness charges our being because for us the vampires are real. They set out into the night to hunt but just for female flesh. There are men out there who are worse than dicks. Oh, Sailor, far worse.

There I was, there we were, away from the safety of street

lights when I saw it, or *him,* as I immediately diagnosed the shape. I took out my phone and started jabbing at it but my shaking fingers couldn't unlock the screen saver. How could I have been so stupid as to wander abroad after dark? Who did I think I was? A man?

I glanced up from the phone. The shape wasn't even a shape, it was just part of the sea that was not glimmering in the moonlight, a blankness, a hole in the reflective surface and Jesus: it was approaching.

I got the screen unlocked but where was the phone icon where was the phone icon where was the phone icon? The blue light had disclosed my position. The figure was pushing something along – wheelbarrow? Shopping trolley? Back and forth through the icons I shuttled on this phone that refused to be a phone.

The figure was not ten feet away when he stopped in my path.

Soldier? What are you doing out at this hour, for fuck's sake?

My friend. His voice welling out of the darkness plucked me from my worst nightmare. It was, in fact, as if he had rescued me from it. The tears were instantaneous.

Oh Jesus. It came out as a whisper. Oh Jesus, you're after giving me such a fright. I bent over the buggy, panting. I thought you were an axe murderer or something.

An axe murderer with a buggy?

I thought the buggy was a . . . I don't know what I thought. I laughed. Relief. Insanity. The surge of fear morphed into hilarity and the note I hit was shrill. I was so pleased to see him, Sailor. So, so pleased. My friend, here, when I most needed him. It was more than relief, more than gratitude. Surely he could see it on my face.

But he could not see my face.

Jesus, I didn't mean to, he was saying, stuff like that. I'm sorry that, I never meant, oh, oh.

No, I'm fine. Another mad laugh, flushing out the fright. I tossed the phone into the nappy bag. So you're stuck out here too in the middle of the night?

Yep. I've been walking for an hour now. She just won't sleep. What about him?

He's teething. Well, I think it's his teeth. He has a fever. I reached into the darkness to place my palm on your forehead. It was cool. My friend was here. Everything was cool.

He peered into your buggy. Hello, you little upstart. Wide awake too, I see.

Wide awake, I confirmed.

Didn't they dose us with alcohol when we were babies? he wondered. How come we don't dose our kids with alcohol?

Do you have any?

No.

That's why.

We were walking by then, my friend and I, for he had turned around to head with me towards the slipway. The tide was out.

It'd be nice, all the same, I said, on a warm summer night like this, to go drinking on the beach.

My friend sighed. Wouldn't it? Just one more time, you know? To be young just one more time.

He spoke with such longing. Mmm, I assented, a lush green flare in my mind's eye, the sunny Eden from which we'd been banished.

Do you ever think they're trying to kill us? he asked.

I do! Slowly. By sucking our energy.

My friend sighed again. Ah, energy. I remember that.

I don't. He has so much of it but I have so little. Ten o'clock at night and I'm a corpse but he's bouncing off the walls.

What was that equation in school – energy cannot be created or destroyed?

It can only be changed from one form to another.

I can't believe you remembered that.

Oh, I have perfect recall of the stuff that happened before he was born, I told him. It's everything since that's a blur.

Because your brain needs energy to make memories.

But they have us dragging our weary bones around in the middle of the night. Although I couldn't help but notice that suddenly I had quite a lot of energy. I felt giddy, in fact, since my friend had shown up. Hey, maybe they planned it together, I speculated. At the playground. Maybe they synchronised their little watches and agreed to keep us both up half the night. Do you think it's a conspiracy?

What, to bring us together?

Well, to kill us, I was thinking.

To bring us together. Had he really just said that? He fell quiet afterwards. We both did. My hand slid up to tug off my scrunchie, releasing my hair down my back, a discreet part of me freed. I was thinking of the old days, which were the new days – these days now are the ones that feel old, jaded, but everything was new back then, everything was tender and full of promise, qualities that seep away over the years. I will have much to tell you when the time comes about how best to live your new days, assuming you will listen. I'll be disappointed if you do.

I didn't risk looking at my friend, just walked alongside him enjoying the sensation of his height, the security it offered. He was my friend. I needed a friend. When it was just you and me, Sailor, day in day out, plodding up and down on our beat, it sometimes felt like we were the last two people on Earth. I would call your father and speak to him in his distant galaxy, the world of offices and office politics, coffee and colleagues, names that meant nothing to me. He sounded so distracted, so remote, murmuring *mmm* and *right* at the wrong points because he was answering emails or glancing over documents or signalling *I'll be with you in a moment* to the person who had just walked in. Cold days were the worst. Should I remind you again how lonely I was, Sailor, how terribly lonely? I didn't know my own mind. I certainly did not know it that night.

Are you happy? I thought about asking my friend, because darkness is liberating on levels that are hard to quantify, being itself hard to quantify. Steep yourself in enough of it and you can see anything you like. In the darkness, my friend could not tell that I was wearing pyjamas under my coat, nor see the dark circles under my eyes. I was a voice by his side and my voice was the one part of me unchanged by your birth. It was the same voice as when I was twenty and suddenly it was saying the same things. Like: dear friend, my dear kind friend who was always good to me, always considerate – are you happy?

He shrugged, or maybe he didn't. What could I see in the dark?

We had come to a stop at the top of the slipway. The beach lay below us, a delicate plain. To set foot on it would be to escalate the energy between us. It could neither be created nor destroyed. Only changed from one form to another. I gave your buggy a hoosh and the two of us were off, *dunka dunka dunka* down the crenulated cement.

The juddering wheels provoked a laugh from the buggy. This was a glorious sound. A laughing child was not a sick child! A laughing child did not have sepsis. The elation made a laughing child out of me. Relief, insanity. Insanity, relief.

In the darkness, the trajectory fell away. The path reconfigured into a new path and here we were, banished from Eden, or were we? My friend had climbed out his bedroom window and I had climbed out mine. Knowing that I had strayed, and that I was straying further still, made me run faster, as if I could outrun my own transgression, shuck it off and ditch it on the beach. He was my friend. I want to say nice things about him. I want to say nice things about friendship. The sustenance it offers does not expire when the friend is absent but continues to radiate, just as that star up there may have burned out years ago. You see it but it may no longer exist. I am getting into areas I barely understand, alternate versions of reality, worlds no less real for being imaginary, like you being there for all of this, right there in the buggy, watching everything that unfolded yet no trace of it will be left in your mind. So can you really be said to have been there at all? *My mother, out running wild in the middle of the night.* What did you do with that information? Where did it go? Fame! my friend yelled at the empty beach, I wanna live forever. It was one of our dumb jokes.

I could feel myself being understood as we walked side by side, could feel my friend's careful fingers probing my depths, open-heart surgery. I welcomed his ministrations. Maybe, just maybe, I told myself as I furiously pushed you along, I should put myself first this once.

Do you remember, I asked my friend because I was seized by a great need to invoke what had been lost, to turn it over in my hands and commemorate it, our heyday. Do you remember when we were young we spent a night drinking on a beach?

Do you remember that bottle of blue stuff, the pride with which we brandished it? Our talisman. Jesus, it was vicious.

Do you remember who else was there? There were a few of us. Six or seven. Their names are gone. Didn't someone try to light a fire with driftwood? Hey, was that you?

Do you remember lying on our backs cupped in a valley between dunes and looking at the stars? Your body ran the length of mine. I could locate you without looking at you. I had sonar for you.

Do you remember the girl you were seeing at the time? Do you remember her name? Me neither.

Do you remember the shooting stars? Three or four of them streaking across the sky in quick succession and us practically yelping at the sight. Never before had I seen a shooting star, and never since. I thought my life would be full of such wonders. Did you? Did you think that too? We were so young.

Do you remember how good it felt, being out that night? Being free.

Do you remember freedom?

He remembered. Of course he remembered. He was my friend.

I pushed and I pushed. I pushed that buggy hard, towards vestiges of the old freedom, the old exhilaration. Running away from her, the drudge, and back to my old self, my real self, traces of whom weaved around us like currents, like those treacherous currents that carry bodies out to sea.

This is me, I declared to you, this is who I am. A woman nightwalking on a beach with her young child who will be a free spirit too if she can help it. What an unreliable witness you were, Sailor, reclining there with eyes wide open. I could tell you anything about that night and you wouldn't know any differently. I could tell you that I stopped then, that it was time to stop running so I stopped. That my friend stopped too, that everything stopped, that it was just him and me looking at each other on the beach. That I reached up to his face, that he reached down to mine. That we placed our hands on something we had lost, and found, that I clung on for dear life to that dear life, that he clung on to me. An outpost, the two of us, whispering to one another on the sand. I could even tell you that my friend wasn't there that night, Sailor, that I pushed your buggy alone, speaking to no one and to nothing other than my own need, which I had allowed to get the better of me. A confounding phenomenon, your presence, if I think about it for too long. Seeing everything but recording nothing. You were not there in a way that night and, in a way, my friend was.

Why is the sand rippled like that? I asked him, although I knew the answer as well as he. Water had pooled in the troughs between the hard winding ribs that had slunk up underfoot like eels.

Strong currents, he told me. His voice was faltering. As was my conviction.

Strong currents, I repeated to myself. Strong currents and weak resolve.

Two girls had drowned on that beach before I was born. My mother warned me about them as a child and now I am warning you. They strayed out of their depth. An undercurrent dragged them down. Your buggy wheels strained against the ridges created by forces hidden beneath the glittering surface of the sea, as dangerous as they are alluring.

Did you know about the two girls who drowned here? I asked my friend, but no one heard me. Not my friend, who wasn't there, not really, unless you count in my head, or my heart, that place where I do my longing, which I do count, it being the most essential part of me. It is the part that made me make you. The beach was abruptly deserted as my friend and his little girl ebbed away to wherever they were, both sleeping soundly I hoped, both dreaming good dreams, I hoped.

I looked into the buggy. Two long-lashed crescents: your eyes were finally closed. A wave of exhaustion hit me too. Were the tide in, it occurred to me with a shiver, we would both have been submerged. Our names carved on a stone anchor lying at the bottom of the sea. 'Oh,' I said in surprise when the buggy lurched sharply downwards.

The front wheels were stuck in a pool of water and my feet, I realised as I tried to reverse the buggy out, were sinking. The tide had turned. Oh yes, Sailor, the tide had turned and we were no longer on dry land, not by a long shot. The sea that moments earlier had sung its siren song was not only advancing but had, I gasped to discover when I looked around, been creeping along the length of the spur it turned out I had been marching across, and by *I*, I mean *us*. I had brought you here, to this spit, or this sandbar – I did not know what to call it, and could not understand how the sea was behind me if I had not passed the sea on the way. Whatever we were standing on would soon be an island and, soon after that, submerged.

The harbour lights seemed unfeasibly far away. How had we strayed that far? I scanned the beach but there was no sign of the slipway, our portal back to the real world, as if it had closed up, sealing us in, or rather out. I turned the buggy around only the buggy would not turn, for the texture of the sand had altered. The texture of the night had altered. You look up sometimes on a sunny day to find an army of storm clouds massing on the horizon. This is the world we live in. Don't talk to me about this world. The trough that the buggy had sunk into was filling with water, which was rising along with my panic. I tried to angle it out backwards but the wheels sank in further and the sand crumbled away underfoot. I hauled and I heaved and finally manhandled it out. A narrow strip of sand led back to the beach, the sea encroaching on both sides.

The sand mounted resistance when tackled in the opposite direction as if a gradient had been added. I applied my body weight to the handle of the buggy. This is how it happens, I remember thinking as I pushed that buggy as hard as I was able. This is how people drown. It wanted us, Sailor. The sea wanted us so it called us. It called me. And I brought you.

The jetty of sand came to an end. Which was like the world coming to an end. Seawater cut us off from the shore. We were marooned on a small oblong island which was growing steadily smaller.

There was nothing for it. I scooped you out of the buggy, oh God, I took my beautiful child into my arms and we plunged into the water.

You woke and cried out when the cold water splashed your bare legs. I didn't have to wade as I'd feared – it turned out it wasn't deep. Then – like something from a parallel dimension – an electronic signal rang out. My phone, transmitting from your father's distant galaxy. It was in the buggy, along with the keys to the house. How ominous it looked in silhouette, a child's buggy abandoned at the water's edge.

The phone kept ringing. I vacillated and then splashed back.

With your weight out of it, the buggy trundled lightly along in our wake as I dragged it with one hand and clasped you to my hip with the other, the phone ringing away. I told you I loved you as I entered the water again as if we were plunging to our death. *I love you, I love you, you're a dear little boy and I love you* while the cold water spattered your skin because you were a helpless little thing at your mother's mercy. *I love you, I love you* morphed into *fucking hell, fucking hell* and then we were through. The phone stopped ringing. The darkness I had revelled in because it hid my tired face had hidden so much more, the truth in particular. Both of us were bawling by then.

I wrapped you in your blanket and clutched you to me, held your cheek to mine, trying to push my love into your bloodstream, or something. Love is the most eccentric property I know of. Endangering it only serves to reinforce it. A disturbance overhead. I looked up to see an angular contraption, mechanical wings – a heron? – and I shielded the crown of your head. It delivered a raucous shriek, serving me further notice that I was out of my element, an interloper in this place.

The first trace of dawn streaked the horizon. Your father had an early start. He would be waking to an empty bed, your empty room, our empty home. I reached for my phone and it started ringing in my hand. Things were happening in the wrong order.

'I'm ringing about your son,' a man informed me.

I whipped around. The beach was empty. 'Who is this?' I asked carefully. The authorities, I was thinking. They were onto me.

'You rang about your son. He has an abscess and a rash?'

'Oh, the doctor!' I exclaimed over your cries. 'Yes, he's better now, thanks.' But that wasn't the end of it. The doctor had questions. Convulsions? Was my son still experiencing convulsions? The raised rash: was it any worse? What about sensitivity to light? 'He's fine,' I kept insisting, your sobbing suggesting otherwise. 'He's fine, everything's fine.' Hate that word.

'The abscess?' the doctor wanted to know.

'It's gone.'

'Gone?'

'I mean, look, he's just teething. It's just really bad teething, okay?

'Thank you,' I said over his next question. 'Thank you so much. Goodnight.'

I hung up, powered off the phone, dropped it into the maw of the nappy bag and zipped it shut like I could disappear the whole shameful mess down there. I bundled you back into the buggy and hurried away from the scene of the crime. So much of parenting is about getting away with it.

Not a sound out of you as I trekked across the sand following not two but one set of wheel tracks, not two but one set of footprints. I located the slipway and slipped past the lifeguard hut, back into the snow globe to the streets of sleeping souls. 'There was this man,' I told you as I began the long journey home, a journey that was going to take many more years than I had allowed for. 'There was this man, this amazing man. His name was David Bowie. That wasn't even his name. He just declared himself David Bowie and then he was David Bowie. Or Ziggy Stardust. Or the Thin White Duke.'

O Captain! My Captain! His lips are pale and still. Bowie died. He sang a song about his death and then he died. Death is a long story, Sailor. So is life. A long, long story that I will tell you over the years allowed to us, or try to. There now, Sailor. There is a kiss for a good boy, oh the best boy, a goodnight kiss from someone who would kill for you, who would kill others, who would kill herself, and did. That night I made another grave error of judgement. I tried to save a girl who had drowned some years ago, bladderwrack tangled in her hair. She drowned before you were born, seconds before you were born, as she brought you into this world. The birds stopped singing for her. But they will sing again. They are birds, and all this love, it has to go somewhere. It can neither be created nor destroyed, only changed from one form to another. That girl, you'd have liked her, but I left her for dead. Had to. This was a woman's job.

EIGHT

And then I asked your father to leave. We will say no more about the brief but painful interlude of his absence in the hope that you were too young to remember it. Even though he was never home, the place just wasn't the same without him.

NINE

Your father slowed as we passed the display table near the door and then he stopped. He released my hand because yes, we'd been holding hands. Holding hands became possible again once you'd outgrown the buggy. There was a little more to it than that. There was a lot more to it than that. Stuff you don't want to know about your parents.

I stopped too but you tugged my other hand. *SALE* read the sign over stacks of folded sweaters in heritage colours and I wanted my husband to buy something, keep the party going.

'They look nice,' I offered.

'Mmm,' my husband agreed.

'Are they wool? They look like wool.'

He nodded at the sign. 'It says they're wool.'

'Make sure they're machine washable.'

'Mmm,' he agreed again but without checking the washing instructions. You tugged harder.

'Or hand-wash at least.' You pulled as hard as you were able. 'Listen, I'll bring this fella to the charity shop and you have a look at the sweaters. If we finish up first, we'll come back here. Otherwise, you'll find us in that shop we passed at the end of the street. The one with the toy guitar in the window.' I pointed in the shop's direction.

'Okay, honey,' he murmured without looking up. He was rooting through the brick-red stack.

'That colour is good on you. You should try that one on.' You tugged me again. 'Do you know the shop I mean?'

'Yeah,' my husband said, though I'm pretty sure he didn't.

'It's the Animal Welfare one, across the street and up.' More pointless pointing: he still wasn't looking.

'I'll find it.'

'Well, I have my phone. Stop pulling me, darling, I'm coming.'

'I not darling. I Superman.'

My husband stopped rifling through the jumpers to look at me. There is something about how he looks at me. As if he were pointing a camera. Although we stood a good fifteen feet apart, a woman ducked her head and apologised as she passed between us. She felt it too. The first time we met, your father levelled that gaze at me and even though I had never laid eyes on him before, I recognised him. That is the only way I can describe it: recognition. The expression on his face, when he came upon me, said: Oh, it's *you*. Because he recognised me too.

I smiled and then the two of us were grinning at one another like in the old days. The new days. 'I love you,' he said across the shop floor.

So of course I had to blink back tears, tears being my only register. We had not looked at each other for so long. We had not recognised each other for so long. In love there is always loss, Sailor. There is no way around this that I can find. There will be a last look. That last look may come sooner than you think. One of us will be left behind. These are the things you accept when you accept love into your life. I let go of your hand to rummage in my bag for my sunglasses until I remembered they were on my head. I flipped them down like a welding mask to shield my eyes. Your hand found mine again and pulled.

'I love you too,' I told him as I was dragged backwards out of there. I love you too, oh God, don't die. Really, I was too old to live at this pitch of emotion. I wanted a cigarette. I hadn't smoked since my teens. But I was a teenager again, for all intents and purposes, an old and knackered teenager. They say you grow wiser as you grow older, Sailor, but, well, don't hold your breath.

Never smoke, by the way. I'm warning you.

We emerged from the shop and I was confronted with the sky. This was more monumental than it sounds. I gaped up at it and thought gosh. It was a picture-book sky, blue with pillowy white clouds. I hope you'll never quite get what I'm going to say next, Sailor, but I had been looking down for so long – at buggies, Velcro shoe straps, the crown of your busy head – that when I did encounter the sky in that manner on that occasion, it came, like my husband's look, as a jolt. It is amazing what you acclimatise to over time. The sky had been there all along – I mean obviously, obviously; I'm hardly casting pearls of wisdom here – but I had been huddled over you for such a protracted period that I had adapted to life without it.

So off we went to check out the toy guitar you had spotted in the window earlier. You cantered along the pavement, Superman cape streaming, excess excitement displaced into your gait. It was like leading a prize colt. Skittish, exquisite. The beauty nature sometimes throws in your path. People – well, female people – smiled as you skittered along. We had done it, we had gotten there, happy family.

The guitar in the window was gone.

'Don't worry,' I said. 'There'll be more toys inside.'

The shop was dank and smelled of dog. There were rails upon rails of tightly packed clothes. A grey-haired older woman appeared through a bead curtain carrying yet more of them.

'Hi there, the guitar that was in the window a minute ago?'

'Gone, love.'

'Oh.' I looked down at you and waited for her to humour you – oh look, it's Superman, or whatever. She didn't.

'Do you have any more toys?'

'Nah, we don't get many toys in. Cloves, mostly.' She was English. She threw her heap of cloves on the counter. 'There's a few kiddie books over there.'

I squeezed your hand. 'Will we have a look?'

You nodded.

We picked out some picture books and brought them over to the lady. She continued sorting through the donations. This took some minutes – hours in toddler time. Her face was grimy and her fingernails and cuticles were ingrained with crescents of dirt.

'Mama?'

'Yes, darling?'

'Is that a witch?'

I clamped your head to my leg and glanced at the woman. If she had heard, she did not let on.

When she was good and ready, she squinted at the books in your hand. 'Free euro, love.'

I unzipped the coin section of my wallet. I did not have three euro. I checked the banknote sleeve. 'Can you take a fifty?' As the question came out, I heard how ridiculous it sounded. Everything in the shop cost a euro or two.

The woman sighed. 'No, my love, I can't.'

'Sorry. I'll ask my husband for money.' Jesus Christ, listen to yourself. I took the books from your hand and placed them on the counter. Amazingly, you did not protest.

Back out on the street, I glanced down. 'You okay?'

You nodded but your giddiness had deserted you. I stroked your hair. Would you remember any of this? You were at the age where events were beginning to leave an imprint.

'Come on, let's find Daddy and see if he has change.'

We made our way along the sunny side of the street then crossed the road through glinting cars to the gentlemen's outfitters. I stood smiling in the direction of the display table while my eyes adjusted to the comparative dimness. I was smiling at no one. The jumpers my husband had rifled through had been refolded and stacked. I led you down to the fitting rooms but he wasn't there either.

The shop assistant looked up from the counter. I don't

know what was written on my face but he was at pains to reassure me that my husband had only just left, that I might even catch him.

'Where's my daddy?'

'I don't know, sweetie. Let's give him a call.'

It went to voicemail. He hated voicemails. I hung up. 'Hey, I know! Let's go into that shop and see if they've anything nice.' I pointed at the newsagent's across the road, which had buckets and spades hanging from the entrance.

I broke the fifty on a Kinder egg. More plastic. Buyer's regret.

On the pavement outside, I got down on my hunkers to explain to you how to purchase things. 'When the lady gives you the books, you give her the money, okay?'

'The witch?'

'She isn't a witch, Superman. You know the way you hate taking baths? That's what happens when you don't. Now.' I crossed your palm with three silver coins and explained that this was your money. 'Moneys,' you corrected me. I gave you pretend books, you gave me the coins. We switched back and did it again. You were delighted with this game. The magic had disappeared along with your daddy but we were going to get it back.

This time there was a dog in the charity shop. 'Oh look: a dog!' I exclaimed for your benefit.

'Aw!' you said. 'He so cute.'

He wasn't, God love him. A dirty white Staffordshire bull terrier with torn ears and a growth on his rear end. Three people were staring down at him. The dog licked his lips and swallowed.

'Well of course 'e's a right andful,' the grimy woman was proclaiming. 'They ain't cut is balls off, mate.' The dog's legs were set at the four corners of his squat body like a butcher's block and indeed they had not cut off his balls.

The woman put her hands on her knees to look into the dog's face. 'They ain't cut your balls off, av they, little feller?' The dog wagged his docked stump of a tail and lifted and set down each paw in turn. Then he contorted to savage an itch on his back with his teeth. The woman straightened up and tutted. 'Fleas. Poor bugger.'

'Poor bugger,' you repeated.

Nobody noticed the adorable thing my child had just said. The books we had picked out were still on the counter. I retrieved them and gave you the nod.

You held the coins up to the woman. She glanced at you then back at the dog. 'It's gonna be tricky finding an ome for an old trooper like you, innit?'

'Aw,' you said again, reaching out to stroke the dog's filthy back.

'Careful,' I said, snatching your hand away. 'Always ask the owner first.'

The dog wagged his stump at you.

'Well, at least 'e seems to be aw-wight wiv kids. That'll make im easier to place but, frankly, I don't fancy is chances. Not with vat fing on is arse.'

'Mmm,' concurred the other two, nodding gravely. One

of them was holding his lead.

The dog licked your hand. You squealed in delight.

'We'll take him,' I said.

The three faces turned to me and I beamed. We could give this dog a happy home! We had a happy home to give. My husband had looked at me that way again. And I had looked at him. A dog would complete the picture. A dog and my child frolicking in the garden. Why hadn't I thought of it sooner?

The Englishwoman narrowed her eyes. 'Where do you live?'

'Well, we're down on holiday.'

She put her hands on her hips. 'I can't check out your ome if you're on oliday, can I?'

'Would you like to see a photo? We have a garden.' I reached into my bag for my phone.

'Av you ever owned a dog before?'

'No. I had a cat.' Poor Ming.

'A cat ain't a dog.'

'Yes, I appreciate that. But she was a rescue cat. I have experience with rescue animals. Plus my husband had a dog.'

'Where is your usband?'

'That's what I'd like to know!'

I laughed, she didn't.

The dog, having established that the witch was the matriarch, relocated to sit at her feet. I can't remember what else I said, but it began to sound lame, even to me. The woman issued statements including but not limited to the following:

'A dog as different requirements to a cat, yeah?

'Av you any idea ow much work is involved wiv a dog?'

'You cannot decide to get a dog on a whim, love, d'yah understand me?'

'It's people like you what—'

Oh look, I can't do regional British accents. I stood there listening to it like an admonished child. 'This my mama!' you told the woman in outrage. 'She lovely mama.'

'I'm sorry, forget it,' I conceded, confirming that I was precisely the class of flake that she was up against. The woman folded her arms and rested her case. A whoop of glee from below.

'Ear, is vat kid givin im chocolate? Facking ell, 'e is an all!'

In your hand was the foil Kinder egg wrapper. The dog was licking your fingers.

'Chocolate's poisonous to dogs!' the woman shouted into your face. 'Chocolate kills dogs!' A stunned blinking of your eyes, then your features crumpled.

'He's barely three!' I objected, scooping you up and bailing you out of there. You were right. She was a witch.

Out on the street, I hunched over the phone trying to see the screen in the sun. My husband still didn't answer. I left a voicemail this time. Our child screaming was the voicemail.

I carted you back into the sweater shop. Your father was still gone.

You kept wailing about wanting your mama as I lugged you through the unfamiliar streets of that market town. I didn't know what you were saying. The car, was all I was thinking. I hope he has at least left us the car. I had entered coping mode and was fixating on the car. If I was to manage without my husband, I would have to learn to cope. To cope, I needed the car.

But did I have my car keys? I set you down on the pavement to search my bag for my car keys. I did not have my car keys. They were back in the holiday cottage. How would I get to the holiday cottage without the car? That's if my husband had left us the car. I needed to think. I needed to sit down for days, for weeks, for the rest of my life and think, but I did not have days, or weeks, or even minutes. I had you. And you were wailing. The same thing over and over. 'He want his mama!'

'I'm here,' I said impatiently. 'I'm right here.'

'No: *doggy*! He want his mama! He gonna die and he want his mama!'

'Aw, pet,' I relented, wiping tears from your cheek. 'Kinder's mostly white chocolate and you only gave him a little. He is a big strong dog. He isn't going to die.'

That gave you pause. 'Doggy not gonna die?'

'Of course not. The lady was wrong to scream at you.'

'She wrong?'

'Yes.'

'Not I?'

'No. The lady was wrong, not you.'

Deep satisfaction at being the wronged party. Know the feeling. 'Did doggy like me?'

'He liked you very much, darling. He wagged his tail and licked your hand.'

'He so cute.'

'He was very cute. Now, let's find the car, will we?'

The sobs subsided and you nodded. I took you by the hand but you pulled yourself free to run ahead then tripped in your new sandals and hit the pavement, a little prostrate Superman, your cape flipped over your head. I helped you up and lifted the cape like a bridal veil to reveal your beautiful face and I kissed your tear-stained cheeks.

Both knees were skinned, pinpricks of blood seeping through, cervical shiver. I picked out a tiny embedded stone with my fingernail before clasping you to me. 'Oh, poor darling.' We rocked back and forth while pedestrians detoured around us. When the tears had eased off, I sat back on my heels and said, 'Hey, look what I have!' I reached into my bag again and produced the picture books.

You took the books with one hand and held out the other, opening your fist to reveal three silver coins.

'Oh.' I took the money. 'Well done, darling! You are just the best little boy in the world!'

'I Superman.'

'Yes. Yes, you are. Can Superman help me find the car?'

We made our way along the lane to the car park.

'There it is!' you shouted.

He had left us the car.

The shadow of the tree under which my husband had parked to keep the interior cool had moved on, and the car now gleamed in full sun. The windscreen reflected the monumental sky, the tumble of white clouds against the elation

215

of blue. I could not see whether he was inside.

I tried to compose myself as we approached hand in hand. Why, out of the blue, had my husband looked at me that way again? The look that was birdsong. You don't notice that the birds have stopped singing until they start up once more. Or you do notice. You notice something's wrong, something is missing, something intrinsic, baby blues, the colour draining from your world. But you acclimatise. You have to. There is too much to do, no time to figure things out. We had postponed our love to a time in our lives when there would be time in our lives, and there was never time any more. So when the birds burst into song again, I could not bear for the singing to stop. They startle easily, though. They take flight. They are birds.

And you with your red cape and the big S on your small chest. Suddenly you were growing up so quickly. Suddenly it was going too fast. We stood hand in hand before the family car like relatives outside an operating theatre. Something was fighting for its life in there and there was not a thing I could do, only pray and wait, wait and pray, that my loved one would pull through. What would I do if the news was bad? 'Ow!' you yelped because I'd crushed your sweet hand.

We'd been confronted by the locked car that time we went to buy your bed in IKEA, stranded in the basement car park. The bed-less, fatherless, family-less family car, the chemical castration. Its emptiness was sickening, a family portrait with one member erased. You bawled in the buggy as I tried to ring him but there was no signal under all that concrete.

Your father and I had come to this place to build your world? It ended here in an underground car park toxic with exhaust fumes. He's gone, I thought, because it seemed to me he had reached the conclusion I had almost reached: that this wasn't working, that this never would.

A car cruising for a parking space stopped and indicated. I shook my head: no, we weren't vacating. You were still clutching the stuffed Dalmatian that I really should have paid for as we passed through the checkouts but we were way beyond that. My husband was gone, everything goes, there was no stopping the tide. My little wicker chair, the one my parents bought on holiday, crushed in some landfill. Artefacts from the dreamtime that is childhood. A world you awake from and can never return to again. *You have the keys*, I texted my husband for all the good it would do. No keys, no husband, no phone signal. Another car stopped speculatively and again I shook my head. The chair's value wasn't for itself but for the event it connected me to, my parents as a young couple in their flares and paisley shirts bearing their toddler aloft out of a shop, an occasion which in my head had turned into a parade down the Main Street of whatever picturesque town they had wandered into, and the locals would have smiled because that, I have learned, is what you do when you see a little kid being indulged: you smile at the parents, you smile at the little kid, you keep the joy going, you forge the happy memory, you shore it up, you nail it down, this buttress against the bad times – the bickering, the fights, the silenced birds – so that the young couple can say,

Do you remember the time we had to cart young miss out of the shop in that chair? Here it was, only here it wasn't. The chair was gone like all the rest of it. 'My daddy,' you sobbed, meaning I want my daddy. Yep, you and me both.

Squeak of tyres on the painted surface as yet another driver stopped. This one beeped like I wasn't right there and didn't have an upset two-year-old in my care. You yelped in fright so I took you out of the buggy, triggering the domino effect: the buggy tipped over backwards weighted down by the nappy bag, the nappy bag spewed its contents because I hadn't closed the zip, your bottle rolled under the car. '*My bockle!*' you shrieked. So I held you to my chest and got down on my knees to fish it out but, like my wicker chair, it was just out of reach. I was about ready to grind my forehead into the concrete floor when '*Wheeeee!*' – a figure had appeared, silhouetted against the IKEA entrance. He was horsing a trolley our way.

'Daddy!' You squirmed to be released from my arms and took off into his.

He caught you and threw you squealing into the air. 'Hey, do you want a big boys' bed?'

'Yeah!'

'The kind you get to build yourself, like Lego?'

'Yeah!'

'You want to go home and help me build your big boys' bed?'

'Yeah!'

'Let's get her loaded up then.' A quick kiss for me. 'I got

the safety rail thing too. And a mushroom.' He held up the toadstool lamp. 'My!' you shouted.

Yes, Sailor. Yours.

He strapped the bed and rail onto the roof rack while I folded and stowed the buggy in the boot. Then he turned to you. 'Do you want to ride the trolley back?'

Wheeeeee! the two of you cried on your way to the trolley dock. Do you remember, Sailor, I heard myself rehearsing as I trotted behind taking photos for the childhood auditor, do you remember the day we paraded you around the IKEA car park on a trolley? 'My bed!' you had bawled until I staggered out of the store but your clever daddy had sneaked away when we weren't looking and bought a bed and told you it was the one from upstairs because not all lies are bad and *wheeeee!* we went tearing around the IKEA underground car park. Relief. Insanity. Insanity. Relief. Fixing things at the last minute is still fixing them. People made way when they saw us coming and *wheeee!* a bloke joined in and *wheeee!* went a woman. They nailed that joy down because that's what you do, so when the wolf huffs and it puffs, your flat-pack world withstands a pandemic.

The sun flashed off the windscreen as we approached the car. 'Ow!' you yelped when I crushed your sweet hand. Blood was trickling down your shin.

The driver's door opened. 'Daddy!' you cried and ran headlong towards him with your wounded knees and your ardent heart. I braced myself for another tumble. Slow down, for God's sake! I wanted to call out to you. Don't be in such a mad rush to grow up. It hurts too much.

You did not fall. You launched yourself, red cape flying, still flying, so even now when I think of you it is with red cape flying because I know

He threw you up into the monumental sky, red against blue, then caught you and pulled me into the hug, you at the centre of our universe, our sun, our son. The smell of one another's hair. All this love. It has to go somewhere. This man about whom I had harboured dark thoughts had not harboured dark thoughts about me.

This man who, when you bent over to discourse upon your bleeding knees – because every injury initiated an inquest – didn't turn to me and say, 'Where are the plasters?' knowing I wouldn't have any. Instead he said, 'Oh dear, let's go to the chemist.' So back down the Main Street of that scenic West Cork town we went, each of us holding one of your sweet hands and swinging you high into the air, red cape, blue sky. 'Is it a bird, is it a plane?' asked an old lad in a flat cap and *No!* we said in unison, *it's Superman!* People nailing the joy down so we could say, Do you remember the time we went on holiday and you kept asking if the woman was a witch? And that dog with the thing on his bum? Extraordinary underbite, or was that another dog? So many dogs. 'Gentle!' I would yell as you ran at them. And yes, she was a witch, but she wasn't a dick because she was protecting the animal world from ours. They are too good for us. We are too bad for them. I mean, you don't remember and you won't remember. But I'll tell you. And keep telling you until it becomes family lore. We swung you the whole way down Main Street and the girl in the chemist made a fuss over your knees, declaring you a brave boy in her lovely soft accent and awarding you a strip of stickers, midnight blue with a smiling gold sun and the word BRILLIANT! emblazoned beneath. Then your father glanced at me to check he hadn't misheard it because yes, you had actually just said you were hungry.

* * *

'What this say?' you wanted to know earlier this evening. I was peeling potatoes.

'Move back from the oven. It's hot.'

You backed up. 'What this say?'

I glanced down. You were holding up a strip of paper but the words were upside down. 'Turn it around.'

You turned it around so I was looking at the back of it.

'No, the other way.'

So you turned the strip the other way around and the right way up. It was those stickers from that holiday, meaning you had pulled some cupboard or drawer apart. There was one sticker left.

'It says brilliant.' I put the last potato on the chopping board. If I cut them up smaller, they'd cook faster. Unsheathed a knife. Cervical shiver.

'What this say?' I glanced down again. Same sticker.

'Brilliant.'

'What this say?'

'It still says brilliant.'

'What this is?' you tried instead and I realised that you wanted to know what it *meant*. I put the potatoes in the pot, the pot on the hob, and poured the kettle of boiling water into it before getting down on my hunkers. 'Brilliant means wonderful, amazing, the best thing ever.'

You climbed onto my lap nearly knocking me over. I sat on the floor and saw us reflected in the oven glass. We were still the most beautiful thing I had ever been part of. I watched you picking at the edge of the sticker with your still-soft fingernails, trying to peel it off the strip, biting my tongue because it was taking so long and I had to clear up the Lego, chop the carrots, get the wash in before the dew fell. The arms of my top and your father's shirtsleeves were cavorting with each other on the clothesline.

'Well done!' I exclaimed when you finally got the sticker off but then it got stuck on the pads of your fingers and I swallowed a curse. You picked it off with your other hand so it got stuck on that hand, then back onto the original fingers. Good luck with cling film. I refrained from intervening because you have to learn to do things for yourself, Sailor, seeing as I won't always be here for you. I will always want to be here for you but there will come a day when

But no matter what addled state my brain is in by then, I will know

All those electrons or whatever it was we shared down the years, what are they called? They don't just stop. Energy cannot be created or destroyed.

A lot of negotiating before you gained control of the

sticker. I was more triumphant about this than you. Your successes mean more to me than my own. That time you won the colouring competition? Nearly burst. 'Mama,' you said formally as you stuck the sticker to my chest, 'you are brilliant!' You threw your arms around my neck. 'I love you more than my puppy.' You didn't have a puppy but anyway.

'When I was in your tummy, was I so cute?'

'Oh my God, you were so cute.'

'Was I really tiny?'

'Yes. When you started, you were this tiny.' I indicated a space of a millimetre or two between my thumb and index finger.

'Was I just a hand?'

I laughed and then we were doing that thing again, our thing: laughing into one another's eyes. All that time I had thought I was jollying you along when all that time you were jollying along me.

I kissed the top of your head. You were getting big now, full head of hair. The toddler tottering about was gone, replaced by this little boy whom I loved even more. Already he was slipping away to make room for the next incarnation, each version of you retreating a step further towards the door until one day you would be gone. Would that I could replace myself so easily. Put someone more evolved in my place. Or revert to who I was before you came along and I regressed. In being unable to articulate my position, I wasn't a million miles away developmentally from you, resorting to screaming to make myself heard. We grew up together, you and I, in a way. And now here we are. In one another's arms. And I know

When you're up there at the podium, accepting your Nobel or whatever, I will know

'I would like to thank my mother,' you had better say.

I have the sticker still, by the way. BRILLIANT! Which I'm not and, chances are, neither are you.

You might be David Bowie though he's a once-off.

You may discover the cure for cancer but it's a long shot.

Maybe you'll arrest climate change. Someone had better, and fast.

The likelihood is you'll be another working stiff in a sea of working stiffs.

The world needs working stiffs.

If you are one such stiff, I will know

Cannot unknow

My grandmother in her nineties, dementia, crying out for the baby, the baby, oh God where's the baby. I get it now. The magnitude. She couldn't unknow either.

Soon, Sailor, probably sooner than I think, you will realise that dressing as Superman is a thing little kids do. You will hang up your blue-and-red suit. And soon after that – again probably sooner than I think – working-man's duds, sea of stiffs, bus home, rain.

Valerian, campion, speedwell, vetch. There are gentle things in this world. Gentle but resilient. Be one of them, Sailor.

Let me tell you about the latest phase this mother of yours is going through: I keep thinking I'm glimpsing faces from my childhood. The kids I went to primary school with, now grown up and passing me on the street. I stop and do a one-eighty. If they recognise me, they don't betray it. I haven't laid eyes on most of them since we were eleven years old. How funny we all looked in our confirmation photo, palms pressed together in holy prayer, some of us dressed in the same outfit – there was so little to choose from back then. Feels like a message, as if I'm beginning to see through the whole thing. The tape is running down revealing the same extras, the same background scenery. Which sounds unsettling but actually it's a comfort. A time that is lost is not lost entirely. Childhood, the past – it's right here.

I tell my husband about my childhood and he tells me about his but it isn't the same. We can never know each other as we were then. But I know you. I will see the child you were in the man you will become. So come to me. When you need me, come. When you are lost, when you are low: come. When the birds have stopped singing, or you have stopped hearing, because they never stop singing. They are birds.

When you have no hair and I have no teeth.

When you have a pot belly and I have whiskers.

When you are stooped and I am buckled. When it's a Beckett play.

When you wear beige anoraks and I wear bed jackets. Permanently, that is. When I am permanently wearing a bed jacket because I am permanently in a bed, and you are on the visitor's chair listening to me witter on,

and on,

I will know

When you are on statins and I am too bewildered to understand that this middle-aged man is my baby.

– Oh, Time is coming for us, Sailor. Time will do us in –

You hardly know what time is

But soon you'll find out.

This nice middle-aged man whom I may or may not recognise. Because my mind may be mush by then. Mush like the food they spoon into me.

I will still look at you and know

Somehow

Maybe through that thing we do? The electron exchange, the pheromones, ion stream?

No idea what I'm talking about. Properties I'll never understand.

Worlds no less real for being imaginary.

When you are ordinary and I am wondering whatever happened to that child of mine

My woodland sprite of a child

My forest fawn

No, not mine, not really

Yet more mine than anything in my life. Mine in a way I would kill for.

You were such a loving boy. So unruly but so loving. I your scarf, Mama, as you threw your arms around my neck.

Why am I talking about you in the past tense?

I encountered an army of mothers at pick-up outside the school that I was sussing out for you the other day. They appeared from several directions at once – around corners, down streets, out of cars. Like zombies, was my first thought as I watched them gravitate towards the school gates. Some of them were pushing buggies, others wheeled scooters, one woman carried a teddy bear. It would be a mistake to assume that because of the soft toy the woman herself was soft. The women carrying teddy bears are the most dangerous of them all. They would kill to protect the owners of those bears. Sailor, I have been that soldier.

I stepped back to allow them to pass. These women were not zombies: they were warriors. Nothing would have stopped them. Nothing would get in their way. Marching to the summons of the school bell, catching the children who ran into their arms. Standing over their young until their young were ready to stand alone. Only then would the warriors stand down. The reason this work is considered unchallenging is that women mainly do it.

Here's more of it: I was born with you. This was news to me. A baby girl is born with all her eggs in her ovaries. How about that? A part of you was always a part of me. I don't want to read too much into this staggering fact but still.

Oh God, where's the baby?

Right here. The baby was always right here. Born carrying the baby inside.

Was I just a hand?

Why are you crying, Mama?

Because everything about you makes me cry.

If you forget who you are – and there will be times when you do – I will remind you, because I know

Vetch. Saw it on the verge today. Smiled.

You may feel defeated.

I hope not.

But you will. You may feel defeated at some point because at some point you will be defeated.

Things may not work out for you.

I hope they do.

But by the law of averages

You will be average. There are seven billion of us on this planet, or is it eight? Ten? We can't all be special.

But I will know

When I'm on a Zimmer frame and you've a bad knee

When I've forgotten my name and you're calling me Mama again, as a prompt as much as anything: *Mama?*

I will know

All this presuming I reach a ripe old age

By ripe I mean rotten, my mind gone

But I'll know

That this middle-aged man

With the grey hair

The no hair

The bald as the day you were born hair

I will always know

Sailor

When no one else knows

Or cares

Oh, someone will always care for you!

Promise me someone will always care for you!

Sailor

My Sailor

For a few years more

When you are staring at me watching the time go because I can't remember the end of my sentence

The way I stared at you watching the time go because you didn't yet know the words for your question

When it's over

When the wind is weaving through the branches

But the tree no longer stands guard over the children

All the scenic children

Those happy beautiful children

The tree is still trembling but the tree is felled

The tree is lying on the forest floor looking up at the new leaves

Those translucent new leaves backlit by the spring sun after a hard winter, such a hard winter, oh, oh

Thinking: all this

I am leaving behind all this

Only this time it's for real.

Speedwell, eyebright, beach flaring white and we never called him Daddy again.

When the birds are singing again

Really singing

Grand-finale stuff

Hadn't thought about death until I had you. A door opened when you entered my life and that door goes two ways. A baby was placed in the crook of my arm, and a skull on my open palm as I was crowned a mother. Here is your baby. One day you will lose him. He will lose you. You will all lose each other, and he never called her Mama again.

I was thinking about you that time in that forest glade when it occurred to me that you were thinking about me. A tiny person was out there thinking about me, a tiny person who smiled when I appeared. Not just any tiny person. My tiny person. I am a mother, I thought then, and got down off my cross. Came plunging out of the undergrowth: *It's great to be not dead!* That blonde woman standing guard over you was likely a mother too. And her apoplectic dog. I'm her now. I'm where she was at. Evidently in control of my life, evidently enjoying it.

When I'm lying there thinking these things

I'll hear the baby crying

Clear as a bell

Oh the baby, I will cry out in panic, *oh God, where's the baby*, and I will try to scramble through the briars, the chest-high mound of briars

out of the bed

the trolley

the hospital corridor

I ploughed through those woods, Sailor. I ran until I thought my heart would burst and then I ran more. 'I'm coming!' I bellowed to that baby, careening down the hill like a Viking because I am the one who knows

Where's the baby!

You will squeeze my hand and say, I'm right here, Mama,

Your baby's right here

I love you more than my puppy, Mama

And I will see my child again, the child you are now, this child.

When I'm lying there thinking that I can't change this world

I'll also be thinking

That you can.

Your father and I on a May morning took each other's hands and said *I do*, sunlight sluicing over us like love, love sluicing over us like sunlight, running whooping along the beach at night, two creatures who had just discovered fire. We were going to try to make a baby, what an act of faith. I had never felt more connected to another human being. *I do*, we said, and we did.

The day you were born, a door appeared. A new room in my life

A whole new wing.

The most beautiful thing I had ever been part of.

When I'm like, Who are you, dear?

And you're like, I'm your Sailor.

I will grope around for my glasses ('They're on your head, Mama') so I can see you as it floods back up, this energy that cannot be created or destroyed. 'Darling, look at you, all grown up!' I will say, reaching out the claw-like hands that never cease to shock me. Come to say hello to me, Sailor? Or goodbye. Loving me like you loved your raggedy old teddy bears. Didn't care what state they were in. Explaining to me how they came alive at night. Worlds no less real. Tormentil, meadowsweet, my hand in my father's, your sweet hand in mine, a little hand perhaps someday in yours. All this love, it has to go somewhere. The Earth rotates beneath us and all is well, for now. We both understand that what we share is temporary. That our time is almost up.

But we shared it. Every disaster, every breakthrough, every scream, every embrace, notching them up like your height marks on the wall until there were no more growth spurts, until there were no more notches, until we reached the end.

Then we discovered that there is no end. Though the birds end, the birdsong does not. New birds sing the old song. *Let's make a baby!* Love will sluice over you like sunlight. Valerian, sea thrift, a beach flaring white. This energy cannot be destroyed.

When you are not who you are

Like I was not who I was,

When you are not you

Like I was not me,

Then I will remind you. I will tell you that once you were a small boy with a great sense of adventure. You smiled at every face that met yours

You were the child who flew into your father's arms, I will say. An airborne child. Red cape, blue sky. Because I will know

That under your shirt

With the frayed collar, the missing button, you raggedy old teddy bear you

You dear old raggedy bear

Under your oily overalls, your fast-food uniform, hopefully not your prison jumpsuit – whatever you end up doing with your life, even if it disappoints us both, I'll still know

Maybe you'll be like David Bowie

Forever cool

Even in that Mick Jagger video

O Captain! My Captain! He didn't make seventy

But I will know that under them, your cool or uncool clothes

Is a little blue suit

With a long red cape

And a big yellow S

S for Sailor

And that this man carries that child inside him

The one who can fly.

I will know this because

I carry him inside me too

Always did

Always will.

Acknowledgements

I wish to acknowledge the funding from the Arts Council of Ireland and Fingal County Council that helped support me during the writing of this novel.

Goodbye to my friend Christine Rossiter (1982–2019) and my cousin Carolan Long (1981–2020), two young mothers who had to leave behind their children. Goodbye to Ruairí Keegan (2017–2023), taken from his loving family by a sudden illness.

My thanks to the following people:

Angus Cargill, my editor at Faber, the pre-press team, Josephine Salverda, Djinn von Noorden and Rachel Malig, and Simon Trewin, my agent.

My sister, Mia Kilroy.

The writers Sarah Bannan, Chris Binchy, John Boyne, Anne Enright, Aoife Fitzpatrick, Carlo Gebler and Paul Murray.

Joseph Lennon, John Immerwahr, and the faculty of Villanova University Center for Irish Studies.

The librarians of Howth and Baldoyle who are part of the village that raises the child – particularly Aideen Daly, Geraldine Egan, Ciara Farrell, Kayla Hertz, Jacinta Judge, Íde Ní Liatháin, Margaret O'Neill, Fergus O'Reilly, Frank Price, Anne Tierney, Derek Wilson, and our guide through children's fiction: Clíodhna O'Reilly.

Alan and Lawrence, my dear ones.